Future Imperfect

Simon Rose

To Tammy Lyn !

Escape into

Your imagination !

Future Imperfect

Simon Rose

TYCHE BOOKS LTD.

Future Imperfect
Published by Tyche Books Ltd.
www.TycheBooks.com

Copyright © 2016 Simon Rose
First Tyche Books Ltd Edition 2016

Print ISBN: 978-1-928025-45-0
Ebook ISBN: 978-1-928025-46-7

Cover Art by Henryca Citra
Cover Layout by Lucia Starkey
Interior Layout by Ryah Deines
Editorial by M. L. D. Curelas

Author photograph: Simon Rose

This book was funded in part by a grant from the Alberta Media Fund.

Alberta
Government

This book dedicated to Maggie and Cole, loyal companions on a magical journey.

Contents

Chapter One
The Storm

THE BASEMENT WAS filled with even more electronic junk than usual. Alex Mitchell, fourteen-year-old technical genius, had been taking equipment apart again. He was particularly skilled at taking computers apart and putting them back together. He'd even built a few computers himself. Alex's best friend and neighbour Stephanie sat across from him at the scratched and battered old dining table. This was where they did all their work together in Alex's basement. It was the beginning of summer vacation and they had plenty to do. Alex's mom, Angela, was always bringing him home obsolete technical equipment that was going to be trashed at her office. Alex had always had an interest in electronics. His dad joked that when Alex had been in his crib if the baby monitor had been too close he'd no doubt have taken that apart too.

Alex started working with old radios, TVs, DVD

players, and small appliances such as toasters before moving on to more sophisticated equipment such as computers, laptops, gaming systems, and phones. Both he and Stephanie were also very skilled with tablets, cell phones, and iPods. Alex had mostly worked alone while growing up. Yet when Stephanie's family moved into the neighbourhood a few years earlier, she and Alex soon realized they had a lot of the same interests. They were both proud to be geeks and nerds, something that made them stand out from the other kids at school. Alex and Stephanie were probably the only students who looked forward to a summer filled not with camps and outdoor activities but with rifling through electronic components in a gloomy basement. They'd even tried developing their own apps and gaming software.

As HE FOCUSED on the motherboard of the computer they'd been taking apart, Alex could sense Stephanie watching him.

"What?" he said, looking directly at her.

Stephanie's fiery red hair was even more unruly than usual. Her freckles were also always more noticeable in the summer months.

"You're such a geek," she said.

"Me? What about you?"

"Sure, I'm a geek too, but you're a big geek. After all, you're the one with the favourite pink screwdriver."

"It's not pink," Alex shot back, indignant. "It's red, and it's only the handle anyway."

"Looks pink to me," said Stephanie, smirking.

"The colour's faded. It's not that new, you know that."

"Geek."

She scowled at him but then followed up with a smile.

It was hardly surprising that both of them were so interested in technology. Alex's dad worked as a developer for Castlewood Dynamics, one of the biggest companies in Silicon Valley. His mom worked in the technical field for the federal government. Stephanie's parents were also both employed by high-tech companies in the area.

"Come on, you two," Alex's dad, Andrew, called from the top of the basement stairs. "We're going to be late."

"I almost forgot about the presentation," said Stephanie.

"Okay, coming," Alex shouted back to his dad.

He and Stephanie were attending a presentation conducted by one of Silicon Valley's leading young software developers. Andrew had managed to get them tickets, despite Alex and Stephanie only being fourteen years old. They put down their tools and stepped away from the table.

"Hurry up," said Andrew, when they reached the top of the stairs. "It's raining like crazy out there. I'll bring the car 'round from the garage to the front."

Andrew hurried outside into the pouring rain as thunder rumbled overhead. The garage wasn't attached to the house so they couldn't reach the car without going out in the storm. Lightning flashed across the sky as Alex and Stephanie quickly put on their shoes.

"Wow," said Alex, glancing outside. "It's really coming down."

"Well, it sure beats having no rain at all," Stephanie remarked. "I know my uncle's been complaining about the farm. There's been no rain out there for months."

"True, this'll be a nice change for him."

Andrew sounded the horn as he brought the car to the front of the house. Stephanie raced over and clambered into the back seat. Alex locked the door to the house with his key then ran over in the rain to join her in the back of the car. They both fastened their seatbelts and Andrew drove away.

ALEX, STEPHANIE, AND their families lived in a neighbourhood just outside San Jose. The presentation they were attending was taking place at a hotel downtown. The rainstorm was getting worse as Andrew drove along the twisting roads near the woods. There wasn't much traffic and only a few other cars passed by on the opposite side of the road. Andrew's windshield wipers were operating at top speed but hardly made a difference to the visibility.

Andrew's phone rang. It was Angela. He touched the screen to answer the call hands-free.

"Where are you?" asked Angela.

"On the road," Andrew replied. "Just taking Alex and Stephanie to that presentation."

"Okay, well, I just got home and John Hartfield called. They got your proposal and they'd like to set up a meeting as soon as possible. Did you only give him the landline number here at home?"

"Yeah, didn't want his number showing up on the Castlewood cell. The company tends to keep an eye on all that. He must have called just after we left. So did he want me to call him back right away?"

"No, he said he'd be tied up at Hartfield Tech for an hour or so, but he'll be at the office until quite late.

I told him you'd probably call him back as soon as you got home."

"Okay, I could do that. Wow, it's really coming down hard here. I can hardly see the road up ahead. Is it raining there as hard as it is here?"

"Yeah, really heavy. Anyway, so you'll call him later? He said he'd be available on his cell until later tonight. He's waiting for your call."

"Yeah, okay. I'll be back as soon as I can and I'll call him."

"Okay, drive safe."

"Will do. Bye."

Andrew pushed the button to end the call.

"What's Hartfield Tech?" Alex asked.

"They're a new company in Silicon Valley," Andrew replied. "They do similar work to what we do at Castlewood."

"Robots and drones and that kind of thing?" said Stephanie, very intrigued.

"Yes, but they're just starting out, so they're nowhere near as big as Castlewood. Hartfield do a lot of research and development, the same as what I do now. I might go and work for them but it's only an idea right now. It doesn't hurt to talk to them."

"Have you talked to Mr. Castlewood about us coming in to the office to see all the labs and testing areas?" said Alex.

"I did, yes. He knows how smart the two of you are, but it's not the right time at the moment."

"But you said we could come."

"No, Alex, I said I'd ask him and that I thought it might be a good idea. Look, he knows you're a very bright prospect for the future, no question there. You too, Stephanie."

"Thanks," she said.

"I'm sure there'll be a time to visit soon," Andrew added.

"But when?" asked Alex.

"Not right now," Andrew replied, firmly. "We're really busy with so many projects at the moment and they're all at a crucial stage. We've got deadlines for the government contracts as well. Hopefully when things quiet down a bit you'll both be able to visit."

Alex and Stephanie looked really disappointed.

"Hey, come on, guys," said Andrew, smiling. "It won't be long, I promise. Man, this rain is something else."

The wipers were still going back and forth at full speed but it was very difficult for Andrew to see the road ahead clearly through the windshield. He reduced his speed as they approached a bend in the road. There were no visible headlights belonging to other vehicles, but suddenly Andrew's car was slammed into from behind. Andrew struggled to control the steering wheel as the car spun wildly toward the side of the road. Alex and Stephanie both screamed as the car collided with a tree on the roadside. Despite wearing his seatbelt, Alex was flung against the side of the car, bashing his head on the doorframe. Stephanie was knocked unconscious by the impact, and Andrew was slumped across the steering wheel.

Alex was only half-awake when he noticed two flashlights approaching the wrecked vehicle. Perhaps someone in the other car was coming over to help? He saw several shadowy figures obscured by the torrential rain as they approached the car and opened the driver's door. Alex also thought he heard a woman's voice.

"Is he alive?"

"Looks like it," said one of the figures.

That was last thing Alex heard before he lost consciousness.

Chapter Two
Unwelcome News

ALEX WOKE UP in a hospital bed. A small needle was taped to the back of his left hand. A plastic tube led to a plastic bag containing saline drip hanging on a metal pole beside the bed. A middle-aged man in a white doctor's coat was checking Alex's pulse and taking his temperature. Angela was sitting beside the bed.

"Where am I? What happened?" said Alex, trying to sit up.

"It's okay," said Angela, gently placing her hand on his arm. "You're going to be fine."

"Calm down," said the doctor, gently removing the needle from Alex's hand. "You've been asleep for a while but you seem to be making a good recovery."

"What about Dad? Is he okay?"

"We don't know," said Angela.

Her voice quivered slightly, and her bright green eyes appeared paler than usual. She looked as if she'd been crying. Angela gently squeezed Alex's hand, her round, friendly face forcing a smile as she held back her tears.

"They haven't been able to find him."

"What do you mean?" Alex asked, scarcely believing what he was hearing. "He was in the car with us. He was hurt, I think, when the other car hit us. I remember some people from the other car were trying to help us. What do you mean they haven't been able to find him? Is Stephanie okay?"

"Yes, just a few aches and pains but nothing serious," Angela replied. "She was in here overnight but her parents took her home this morning."

"What time is it?" said Alex.

"Almost five," the doctor replied. "I think we can send you home. If you feel dizzy or anything like that, be sure to get to a clinic."

He turned to Angela.

"I think he'll be fine after a good night's rest, but keep an eye on that head wound. We'll need to see him again for a check-up in a couple of weeks. You can give us a call to set up an appointment once you know your schedule, no worries. If you can just stop by at the desk and complete the discharge paperwork."

The doctor left the room.

"How did I get here?" asked Alex. "And where's Dad?"

"Luckily, a truck passing by found you and Stephanie unconscious in the car at the side of the road. They called an ambulance and the paramedics brought you here."

"But where's Dad?" Alex repeated.

"Like I said," Angela replied, calmly. "We don't know. The car keys were still in the ignition and his wallet was on the floor but there's no sign of him. There are some police officers here, Alex. They'd like to talk to you before we go home."

"What about?"

"Just some questions about what happened and if you remember anything. They already chatted with Stephanie earlier but she doesn't recall anything after the car hit the tree."

Angela went over to the door and opened it. A male and a female police officer stepped inside.

"Hello, Alex," the woman said, smiling.

She extended her hand and Alex shook it gently.

"I'm Officer Marino, and this is Office Henderson."

Marino had short dark brown hair and kind brown eyes. Officer Henderson had short cropped black hair and wore a much more serious expression.

"I'm glad you're feeling a little better," said Marino. "We won't take up too much of your time. I'm sure you're ready to go home."

"If you can just tell us a little more about what happened," Henderson added. "Anything that might be of help in our investigation."

"Where's my dad?"

Officer Marino looked over at Angela, who nodded.

"We don't know, Alex," replied Marino. "There's no sign of him at the point on the road where the car was hit."

She glanced over at Angela again before continuing.

"We think he may have been kidnapped."

"Kidnapped?" said Alex, in astonishment.

"It's just one of the leads we're following," said Henderson. "We spoke to Robert Castlewood earlier today. He agreed that, based on your dad's recent work on some highly sensitive projects at Castlewood Dynamics, kidnapping's a real possibility. Can you tell us what you remember about the accident?"

"It was really raining hard, I remember that," Alex began. "My dad could hardly see through the windshield. He'd just finished speaking to my mom on the phone."

"Were there any other cars or other vehicles around?" Henderson asked.

Alex shook his head.

"No, we didn't see anyone on the road, but then another car came out of nowhere. It must have skidded on the wet road or something. It hit us from behind and my dad was trying to steer but then we hit that tree. I remember banging my head against the doorframe. I saw my dad wasn't moving in the front seat."

"Do you remember seeing anyone else?" said Henderson.

"I'm not sure," Alex replied. "I was only half-awake. I think I saw some people with flashlights. I remember thinking that it must be someone who'd stopped to try and help. They opened my dad's door and they were talking, but I don't remember what they were saying."

"That might have been the people from the truck that found you or the paramedics," said Marino

"I think one of the voices was a woman's, but I really don't remember, sorry."

"That's fine, Alex," Marino replied. "I know this is difficult for you."

"Anything else?" asked Henderson.

"No, that's all. I blacked out after that until I woke up here."

"Thanks, Alex," said Marino, smiling at him once again. "And thanks, Mrs. Mitchell. This might be of help. If you think of something else, Alex, please get in touch."

She placed a business card on the table beside the bed.

"We'll be in contact, Mrs. Mitchell," said Henderson, "about when you should come down to our office. Thank you again for all your cooperation at this difficult time."

"Thanks, Alex. Get well soon," Marino added.

She and Henderson left the room and headed down the hospital corridor.

"Okay, let's get you out of here," said Angela. "I'll go and fill out this paperwork while you get dressed. The front desk's just outside—you'll see it right away. I'll wait for you, okay?"

She gave Alex a brief hug and a peck on the cheek.

"Get dressed and I'll see you out there."

ONCE ANGELA HAD left the room and closed the door, Alex climbed out of bed. He was a little unsteady on his feet but attributed that to the fact that he'd been in bed for a while. He also figured he was probably still feeling the effects of medications and painkillers. Alex's clothes were in the narrow closet, carefully hung there by Angela while he was sleeping. He quickly got dressed, taking care to pull the shirt over his head gently to avoid disturbing the dressing covering his wound.

Once he was dressed, Alex looked at himself in the mirror. The dressing was quite small, and he hoped that the wound wasn't that severe. His thick brown hair was a tangled mess, and in the absence of a comb or brush he smoothed it down with his hands as best he could. His blue eyes were remarkably bright although he had to admit he looked exhausted.

Alex yawned as he reached for his shoes. He sat down on the bed, slipped his feet into his shoes, and tied the laces. He stood up and grabbed his jacket from the closet. With a final glance around the hospital room, Alex picked up the police officer's card from the table. It had Officer Marino's name, phone number, and email, as well as the crest of the local police department. Alex slipped the card into his wallet and went to meet Angela at the front desk.

Chapter Three
Curiouser and Curiouser

ALEX INITIALLY TOOK things easy once he got home, as his mother insisted. He spent most of his time on the couch watching TV or playing games on his laptop. Stephanie visited him much more often than usual. They never talked much about Andrew's disappearance but Stephanie's presence had somehow helped Alex to cope more easily with what had happened.

Andrew remained missing. As far as the police were concerned, there still hadn't been any further clues and no ransom demands from potential kidnappers had been received. It was as if Andrew Mitchell had disappeared off the face of the Earth. The situation had been especially hard on Angela, although she attempted to hide her feelings from Alex whenever they were alone together. Yet he could tell that she was suffering, not knowing one way or the other about Andrew's fate. Alex didn't really know what to think, except that he couldn't bring himself to believe that his dad was dead. It was just too painful to contemplate.

A week after the accident, Alex and Stephanie resumed working in the basement on their many different projects. Alex had been able to remove the dressing from his wound. It had more or less healed but had still left a nasty scar on the right side of his forehead.

"So how are you feeling?" asked Stephanie.

"Not bad," Alex replied, gently touching the scar. "There's been some weird stuff going on here though. I figured it might be because of all the thunderstorms we've been having."

"What do you mean?"

"Power fluctuations, Internet not connecting, weird blips, you know. I'm sure you've noticed them."

"No, not really. What kinds of things do you mean?"

"The TV switching channels on its own then the remote not responding. It fixed itself but sometimes it would go to channels I didn't even know existed."

Stephanie shook her head.

"I've not seen anything like that."

Alex frowned.

"Really? It happened a few times every day when I was relaxing on the couch when I first got back from the hospital."

"No, everything's been fine at our house."

"Well, that's weird. It's probably something to do with our connection with the cable company or something like that."

"Yeah, maybe."

"Have you had any power outages?" Alex asked.

"When it's really hot and everybody's using their air conditioning I've heard that it can affect the local power supply."

"We've had nothing like that at our house either. What's been happening here?"

"Only little things," Alex replied. "I've had to reset the microwave clock because the power went out for a short time. Same with the landline, and my mom had to re-record the voice mail and then reset the date, that kind of thing. We've had a lot of spam phone calls too, and there usually haven't been any of the callers' numbers displayed on the phone."

"Well, everyone gets those," said Stephanie. "At our house we usually don't answer if we don't recognize the number."

"Same with us, but I answered one when my mom was at work. My cell was dead and the battery needed charging. I figured she might be trying to call me on the landline. I answered the call but there was only crackling and what almost sounded like someone's voice. When it stopped though it didn't sound like someone hanging up."

"I wouldn't worry too much about it," said Stephanie, smiling.

"I've noticed a few odd things down here in the basement too, like some of the computers turning on."

"Well, some of them are plugged in, Alex."

"Yeah, but they were turned off at the computer and the monitor."

"So? We could have just forgot. There's so much stuff down here, after all. Could your mom have done something?"

"I doubt it. She hardly ever comes down here. A

couple of nights ago, I was working on that old gaming console and the computer over there switched on."

He pointed at an older desktop model that was standing on top of one of the workbenches.

"Could it be caused by something that was left on at your mom's work?"

"That crossed my mind," Alex replied. "Even though they wipe those clean before they let them leave the office, there could be something they missed."

They went over to the computer, and Stephanie turned it on. They waited for the screen to open and both noticed a video file on the desktop.

"I'm pretty sure that wasn't there the last time we had this computer working," said Alex. "Do we open it?"

"It could be a virus or something."

"Well, if it is, we're just trashing this computer anyway, and it's not connected to anything else here at the house."

They opened the file and immediately had to mute the volume on the computer as the screen filled with static. The video only lasted for fourteen seconds then stopped.

"What was that?"

"No idea. Like you said, it must be something that was left on there from mom's office that they forgot to remove."

"Shall I delete it?"

"Yeah, just send it to the bin."

Stephanie moved the file to the trash then emptied the bin completely to be on the safe side.

"Where's your laptop?"

"Upstairs in the kitchen. Why?"

"Just curious," Stephanie replied. "We could check the news to see if this kind of thing has been happening anywhere else locally. With the TV, I mean. The computer thing's pretty weird but that's probably just something the people at your mom's work forgot to erase."

THEY WENT UPSTAIRS into the kitchen, where Alex's laptop was on the table.

"Mind if I take a look?" asked Stephanie.

"Sure. Want a drink of something?"

"Thanks, iced tea if you have any."

Alex went over to the fridge and took out a jug containing the iced tea. He took two glasses from the cabinet and then grabbed some ice from the freezer. He added the ice to each glass, poured the drinks, and took them over to the kitchen table.

"Are you having online issues too?" asked Stephanie.

"No, why?"

"It says there's no connection to the Internet."

"It was okay this morning."

Suddenly the desktop opened, and the laptop displayed Alex's preferred home page.

"Okay, it's working now."

Stephanie typed in "power outages in San Jose" and hit the search button. However, the screen abruptly became blank again. The home page then briefly reappeared before the screen began flickering between different websites at a bewildering speed. There also static coming over the speakers, similar to that which they'd heard in the basement on the older computer. Then as quickly as it began, the online connection crashed again.

"This isn't that old a laptop, is it?"

"No, a couple of years, that's all."

They were both startled when the TV suddenly came on in the sitting room.

"That's what it did once before," said Alex.

He and Stephanie went into the sitting room. The channels were changing rapidly, completely at random.

"What's wrong with the TV? Is it an old one?"

"No," said Alex, pressing all the buttons on the remote to no avail. "We only got it last fall, around my dad's birthday."

Although the images flickered across the screen very quickly, they were from channels neither Alex nor Stephanie recognized. They moved at an ever-increasing pace before the TV shut off and the screen went blank.

"What happened?"

"The power's out," said Alex. "Look at the microwave."

As Stephanie glanced over into the kitchen, the microwave clock came back on, although the flashing display numbers indicated the wrong time. The landline by the couch also had flashing zeroes on its display. Alex pressed the remote to turn on the TV. It showed one of the local cable stations, and when he checked a few other channels, they all appeared to be fine.

"This is really weird, Alex. Your mom should get someone from the cable company to come over and check it out."

"Yeah, I'll tell her tonight."

Chapter Four
The Visitors

THE NEXT DAY Alex and Stephanie were watching TV in the sitting room when the front doorbell rang.

"Alex, can you get that?" Angela called from upstairs.

Alex stood up from the couch and went over to answer the door. He opened it and saw Robert Castlewood standing on the doorstep with a blonde woman who appeared to be in her early thirties. Robert had thinning grey hair and wore thick-framed glasses. He looked as if he'd just come straight from the golf course. His short-sleeved shirt displayed the small crest of one of the city's most exclusive golf clubs. The woman, however, was impeccably dressed in business attire. She wore a navy blue jacket and skirt and a white blouse. Her hair was swept back from her face and fastened in a tight bun.

"Alex," said Robert, smiling. "How are you? Why,

you're looking more like your dad every day. How are you feeling? Your mom said you were hurt in the accident."

"Not bad, thanks," said Alex, touching his forehead. "It's a little better now."

"And who's this?"

Alex turned to see that Stephanie was standing just behind him.

"This is my friend, Stephanie," Alex replied. "She lives in the neighbourhood."

"Oh, you must be the girl who was in the accident too. I'm Robert Castlewood."

He extended his hand and Stephanie took it gingerly.

"Are you okay now?" Robert asked. "I heard that you were in the hospital as well."

"Yes, thank you," Stephanie replied, smiling.

"Robert," said Angela, as she arrived at the foot of the staircase. "I thought I heard your voice. Please, won't you come in?"

"Thanks, Angela," said Robert.

He and the young woman stepped inside and closed the door.

"This is Veronica, my niece," said Robert.

"Pleased to meet you," said Angela, stepping forward and shaking Veronica's hand.

Veronica's oval face barely moved as she produced a thin smile.

"I'm sorry to hear about what happened," said Veronica. "I don't know Andrew that well. I've only just started working at the company offices here in California. I've heard a lot about Andrew and his work though. He'll certainly be missed."

Angela gasped, and her face almost turned white.

"I mean, we miss him at the company," Veronica continued. "I'm sorry, I didn't mean to imply that . . ."

"That's fine," said Angela, recovering her composure. "Really. None of us know what's happened yet."

"It must be so hard for you," said Robert.

"Yes," said Angela, "but we're coping with everything. The police have been very good and have given me regular updates, even if there's nothing new to report. Won't you come and sit down?"

For a fleeting second, Alex thought that Veronica's voice sounded familiar but he couldn't place it. Then, as suddenly as it had appeared, the thought was gone.

THEY ALL WENT through to the sitting room. Stephanie grabbed the remote from the coffee table and turned off the TV. Robert and Veronica sat beside Angela on the couch. Robert occasionally held Angela's hand to comfort her as she spoke. Alex and Stephanie sat in the armchairs opposite the couch.

"Did you know that Andrew and I were going to do the charity half-marathon?" said Robert.

"Yes, he'd mentioned that," Angela replied. "He was really looking forward to it. As you know, he just turned forty-five. He figured it was time he started looking after himself a little more. He'd talked about becoming a member of my gym too."

"Some people have said I shouldn't do a half-marathon at my age," said Robert, "but it's for such a worthy cause. As a sixty-year-old man, I'll have to take it a bit easier soon, but my doctors have told me that I'm in good enough shape. They said I have the heart of a teenager."

"You'll probably live forever, Uncle," said Veronica, smiling.

Robert laughed.

"Well, perhaps so, but I'll eventually retire. That's actually why Veronica's here, Angela. I'm grooming her to take over at Castlewood Dynamics."

"Really? Andrew never mentioned anything."

"Well, it's nothing official. Veronica hasn't even said yet if she'd want the job, have you, Veronica? But at least this will help her to ease into things, get a good idea of about how the place works, as well as learning all about our company philosophies and business practices. As you know, I've always been a firm believer in Castlewood Dynamics trying to give something back. I've been very lucky to be so successful and think it's my duty to try and help others in the community."

"Yes, as long as the company's affairs are attended too, that seems like a very reasonable goal," added Veronica, with another thin smile.

She was very cold and businesslike, in marked contrast to her uncle, who Alex knew quite well. He'd come to regard Robert as a kind, grandfatherly figure.

"Typical Veronica," said Robert, with a grin. "Always thinking about business."

"So you're going to retire?" Angela asked.

"Not yet, but I'm thinking about it. I'll probably just take more of a back seat in the coming years and let Veronica do more of the work. We'll see."

ROBERT AND VERONICA chatted with Angela about Andrew for the next ten minutes or so. Alex and Stephanie didn't say much. Each of them merely answered questions whenever the others felt the need to bring them into the conversation.

"Anyway," said Robert, eventually, "we should get going. You can come with us to the office and get those things of Andrew's from the lab. The police didn't want to take anything away and said you could come and collect them. They're not saying that Andrew might be dead, of course. They'd just rather that you have everything for safekeeping at the moment. Veronica can drive you home, if you like."

"Actually, I do have a few errands to run," Angela replied. "I can follow you in my car."

"Well, if you're sure," said Robert.

They all stood up from the couch and walked over to the front door.

"Oh, by the way," said Veronica, as they stood in the doorway. "Do you mind if we take Andrew's laptop, the one he used for work? Do you have it?"

"Yes, it's in his office upstairs," Angela replied.

"Thank you," said Veronica. "There are just a few things that he was working on that we need to shut down. We just need to make sure it's all secure."

"We've done most of it at the office," Robert added. "Very sensitive stuff, some of it with all these pending government contracts. There's probably nothing important on the laptop but we still need to be certain."

"Okay," said Angela. "I'll be right back."

She hurried upstairs to Andrew's home office.

"Now, Alex," said Robert, once Angela was out of earshot. "You make sure that you let me know if there's anything that you need. You too, Stephanie. We're still looking forward to having you visit us at company headquarters once things have quieted down a little. And you need to be strong for your mom too. I'm sure the police are doing all they can, but she needs you to lean on now. Make sure you're always there for her."

"I will, thanks," Alex replied.

"Here it is," said Angela, as she returned to the front door.

She handed Andrew's laptop to Veronica.

"Thank you," she said. "I'll have a look at the files and anything else that's relevant as soon as we get back to the office. I'll be sure to let you have this back by tomorrow at the latest."

"That's fine," said Angela. "Whatever you need to do."

"Now don't forget what I said, Alex," said Robert. "Anything you need, give me a call. You too, Stephanie."

He gave them a broad smile before he and Veronica walked over to their Mercedes parked in the driveway. Angela quickly grabbed her car keys from the kitchen counter before returning to where Alex and Stephanie were standing in the doorway.

"Okay, you two," she said. "I won't be too long."

She hurried to her car and Alex gently closed the front door.

"WELL, THAT WAS good of them to come around," said Stephanie.

"Yeah, Robert really likes my dad. He thinks he's got a lot to offer the company. Robert phoned right away to see if we were doing okay. I think this is the first time he's had the chance to come here in person. He's a pretty busy guy."

"His niece seems a bit cold though."

"Yeah, I've never met her before. I didn't even know he had any family other than his wife that died a few years ago."

"Well, she must know what she's doing if he's going to let her run the company for him."

"I guess."

"Anyway, I'd better go home," said Stephanie. "My mom texted me to say supper's nearly ready."

"Okay. I'll text you later," said Alex. "Which reminds me, I'd better charge my phone."

Stephanie went over to the front door to put on her shoes. Alex went into the kitchen. When he connected the charger to the outlet, the phone screen lit up as usual. Alex was about to walk away when he noticed an unusual icon on the screen. It was in the bottom right hand corner, and he'd never seen it before. He'd heard about things being downloaded to phones automatically when new software was developed. But for some reason the icon really grabbed his attention. It was nothing out of the ordinary, merely a simple, thin circle with the letters *AM* in the centre.

Stephanie called him from the doorway.

"Okay, I'm going."

Alex didn't respond as he intently studied the icon.

"I said, I'm going," she called again. "Alex?"

Stephanie stepped into the kitchen.

"Here," said Alex, beckoning her over to the counter. "Take a look at this."

"What?"

"On the phone," he said, showing her the screen. "It's some kind of app. Have you seen this one before? Is it something new? Like a shopping thing or something like that?"

"No idea," replied Stephanie, as she examined the icon. "It's not one I've seen before. If it's new, it'd be on my phone too, since we have the same model from the same year."

"I wonder what it is?"

"Open it," said Stephanie. "Let's have a look."

Alex shrugged and pressed the app's icon. It opened to reveal a low quality image that had *A. Mitchell* written beneath it.

"Dad?" Alex gasped, in astonishment.

He and Stephanie were both startled by the sound of a message alert. A small green light began pulsing underneath the picture. There was a text message.

Chapter Five
Texts From Tomorrow

"IS HE TELLING you where he is?" said Stephanie, staring at the image on the phone. "Has your dad been kidnapped?"

"I don't know," replied Alex, as he opened the message.

They read the text together.

Turn on the TV to the local news channel. There's a story about volcanic eruption in Indonesia. While the reporter is talking to the camera, a helicopter will be destroyed by the eruption.

"That's weird," said Alex.

"What does that mean?" said Stephanie. "Is it some kind of coded message?"

"How the heck do I know?" said Alex, with some irritation. "It's just a message. I don't know what it means."

"Let's find out."

Stephanie grabbed the remote, turned on the TV, and switched to the local news channel. Just as the text message had said, there was a news report concerning a volcano that was erupting in Indonesia. A reporter was standing in front of the camera telling viewers what had happened so far and how the volcano could erupt violently at any time. He was explaining how the local population had been evacuated and how the emergency services personnel were working at the scene. There were mountains in the background. One peak in the centre of the picture was emitting wisps of smoke but these were nothing like the huge ash clouds normally associated with a volcanic eruption. Alex had his phone in his hand and rechecked the message to make sure that he'd read it correctly. When he looked back at the screen, a helicopter flew in from the right and hovered over the volcano. Alex and Stephanie were shocked and stared wide-eyed at the TV as a huge ash cloud blasted from the volcano. The cloud destroyed the helicopter, which fell from the sky in flames and tumbled down the mountainside.

"Oh, my God," Stephanie gasped.

Alex was silent. His phone vibrated and then emitted a message alert. There was another text.

Did you see the helicopter crash?

"What is it?" asked Stephanie.

Alex handed her the phone.

"Are you going to reply?"

"No. I mean, I don't know. We have no idea what this is about. Anyone could have sent this message. It could even be someone in a different time zone who's already seen this footage."

"Not really," Stephanie pointed out. "The people

30

on the TV said this is live coverage. Everyone would have seen that crash at the same time."

The TV station was replaying the crash footage. Alex's phone vibrated. Beneath the image of the man, the phone's green light was pulsing. There was another message, this time with a live video. Alex's hand was trembling as his finger pressed the icon.

"Hello, Alex," said a man, as the video opened. "I haven't seen that face for a long time."

THE MAN WAS sitting in a room cluttered with computers and scientific equipment. He bore an uncanny resemblance to Andrew, but Alex instantly knew it wasn't his father.

"Who are you?" said Alex. "Why are you contacting us? Do you know where my dad is?"

"And how did you know about the helicopter?" asked Stephanie.

"One thing at a time," said the man. "I knew about the helicopter because to me that's history."

"What do you mean?" said Alex.

"That happened a long time ago. I just had to make sure that I had the exact time and date so I could direct you to the news story."

"I don't understand," said Stephanie, shaking her head.

"I'm contacting you from the future," the man explained.

"Who are you?" said Alex. "Is this some kind of scam?"

"This is going to be hard to believe," said the man, "but my name's Alexander Mitchell. I'm you, Alex."

"What?"

"I'm your future self. That's why I knew exactly

where the two of you would be today and how I could contact you."

"Is this a joke?" asked Alex.

"Maybe we should call the police and give them all the details," Stephanie suggested.

"It's not a joke, Alex," insisted Alexander. "I wish it was, but this is deadly serious."

He pushed back his thick mop of hair to reveal a scar on the right side of his forehead.

"This is the scar I got from the car accident in the rainstorm."

Alex instinctively reached for his own recently healed wound.

"I'm afraid it doesn't heal that well," said Alexander. "At least I've been able to cover it up with my hair all these years."

"That's the same as yours," said Stephanie. "Both scars—even the same curved shape."

"That doesn't prove anything," Alex corrected her. "He could have got that from any kind of accident. It doesn't prove he's me. That's crazy."

"You're in grade nine now, right?" asked Alexander. "I could tell you a few details of how your studies are going to go in the next couple of years, but I can't influence your fate like that. It wouldn't be right. You're on the basketball team for the first time this year. Last year you went on a sailing trip with the school."

"That doesn't prove anything either," said Alex. "I've hacked people's accounts on Facebook and other social media sites. So has Stephanie. You could easily get that kind of information."

"Ah yes, social media," said Alexander, with a chuckle. "I remember Facebook and all those others before they disappeared. They seem like antiques now. Some people don't even remember those kinds of things these days."

"You're right, Alex," said Stephanie. "He could have hacked that stuff. We should definitely tell your mom if we're not going to the police."

"I still have this," said Alexander, holding up a small screwdriver and showing them the handle. "It's not pink of course, Stephanie. The colour just faded with time, even more so by now."

"Alex, is that—"

"It could be a fake," Alex interrupted her. "Just like everything else he's saying."

"Do you remember that big yellow truck you had when you were six?" said Alexander. "How you broke the wheel and blamed it on your friend? Or that sick stray cat you secretly nursed back to health in the backyard and never told your parents about when you were nine? Then there was that time . . ."

The image on the screen abruptly began to break up then it was gone.

"Alex?" said Stephanie. "Are you okay?"

"Yeah," Alex replied, his voice shaking slightly. "Yeah, I'm fine."

"Is it true what he said? About that toy and the sick cat?"

"Yes, yes it's true," said Alex, impatiently. "But how could he know that?"

"Maybe he's telling the truth."

"But it's impossible."

There was a new phone message from Alexander. Alex opened it.

"I'm sorry about that," said Alexander. "It's such a poor connection at times, trying to link with the obsolete technology of your time. I'm sure you noticed some weird things with your laptop and the TV, as well as that old computer in the basement. I was trying to connect but couldn't quite get things to work properly. I hope we can stay connected long enough so that I can tell you everything that you need to know. I can see you both still need convincing that I'm telling the truth. What time does it say on the clock on the microwave in the kitchen?"

"6:10," Alex replied. "Why?"

"Let me make a prediction. At 6:12, the phone's going to ring. It will be your mom telling you she's going to be longer than she expected. She's calling at your grandmother's on the way home. You and Stephanie should order pizza since she won't be home in time to make dinner."

"How could you know that stuff?"

Alexander simply smiled.

"That's not all. When you put the phone down, Stephanie will get a text from her friend Madison. It'll include a funny picture of a cat and the text message will say "lol just like streaky." I assume that's the name of your cat?"

"Her cat, actually," Stephanie replied.

"Okay, whatever," said Alexander. "Either way, that's what's going to happen."

"Why should we believe you?" said Alex. "It's so crazy and—"

The phone rang. Alex and Stephanie both looked over at the microwave clock. It was 6:12. Alex put his cell phone on the counter and walked over to the landline.

"Hello," said Alex very quietly, as he answered the call.

"Alex?" said Angela. "Is that you?"

"Yeah, sorry. Hi, Mom."

"Are you okay?"

"Yeah, I'm fine."

"Okay, good. Can you order pizza for dinner? Buy two if Stephanie's still there. We can always have leftovers tomorrow. I'm calling at Grandma's house on the way home. I just need to see how she's doing with all this stuff with your dad."

Alex was very quiet as he listened to his mom tell him exactly what Alexander had claimed that she would say. Angela asked Alex several times if he was feeling okay before the call ended. As Alex put down the phone, Stephanie almost dropped her cell phone when she was startled by a text alert.

"Oh, my God," she said softly, staring at her phone.

Alex went over and saw the text with the cat picture and the exact wording, precisely as Alexander had predicted.

"Okay," said Alex, picking up his cell phone to resume the video conversation with the mysterious Alexander. "You've got our attention. What's this all about?"

"Robert Castlewood and Veronica were just there, weren't they?"

"Yes," said Stephanie.

"And did she take the laptop?"

"She did," said Alex, frowning. "She said they had to examine it back at the office in case there's any sensitive material on it. She said she's bringing the laptop back tomorrow."

"Her taking the laptop is what sets everything in motion," said Alexander, grimly. "This is where it all begins. Veronica Castlewood must be stopped. It's a matter of life and death for millions of people in the future."

Chapter Six
Learning Curves

"I KNOW THIS sounds insane," said Alexander, "but let me try and explain as much as I can. Stephanie, can you connect the phone to your tablet please, so you can watch the video on there."

"Sure," said Stephanie.

She walked over to the dining room table to grab her tablet. Once she'd connected it to the phone, Alexander continued.

"Is that better?" he asked. "Is the picture a little sharper?"

"Yes, it is," said Alex.

"In the future I'm able to access all the personal records of just about anyone," said Alexander. "It's based on all the interconnections between the web, phones, and so many other sites. It's not 100% accurate and the system has some flaws, but it's still reasonably reliable. That's how I'm able to piece together events, such as your mom's phone call and

Stephanie's text. Of course, I also remember the conversation and events from when I was younger."

"How are you able to access all that information?" Stephanie asked.

"All that training in hacking accounts when I was a kid, I guess," replied Alexander, with a wink.

"Can you tell us more?" said Alex.

"I can, but not now. I might not be able to maintain this connection for long. I'm always potentially under surveillance here. The signals are all scrambled and rotated, but I might have to shut things down without warning. I promise to explain more to you later but there are some things that are very important for you to know. How much do you know about what kind of work Dad does at Castlewood Dynamics?"

"I know it involves robotics and really cool technology but not all the details," Alex replied. "Well, apart from how Dad developed advanced robots that eventually could be used to do many of the regular tasks currently done by people."

"Sounds like a great idea," said Stephanie.

"Yes, it does," Alexander agreed. "It allows humans to do more worthwhile things, but it also has very sinister applications."

The video started to break up, but this time Alexander somehow managed to stabilize the transmission.

"Like what?" Alex asked.

"I don't have time to tell you everything right now in case I lose the connection," replied Alexander. "You need to know that Veronica's arrival at the company made Dad suspicious of her motives with regards to the technology they were developing. He was planning to leave Castlewood and join Hartfield Tech."

"Didn't your mom and dad talk about that in the car on the phone?" said Stephanie.

"Yes," Alex replied. "But Veronica said that she's only recently started working for the company and Robert's not retiring any time soon. That's what he said when he was here anyway. Veronica's not in charge of Castlewood Dynamics."

"I'm afraid Robert doesn't have long to live," Alexander said, calmly. "He's going to die at 1 pm tomorrow after collapsing on a golf course. This is just one of the key events that sets things in motion."

"But he said he was really healthy," said Alex. "He'd just visited the doctor."

"And he was going to do that half-marathon," Stephanie added.

"Unfortunately, it's true," said Alexander. "Or at least it will be tomorrow, and Veronica's responsible."

"What do you mean?" Alex asked. "She's involved in his death?"

"She's also responsible for Dad's disappearance," replied Alexander. "You need to get his laptop back."

"But we have no idea where it is," said Stephanie.

"You'll find it in Veronica's office at Castlewood Dynamics," Alexander replied. "She won't be there tomorrow morning, so you should be able to collect the laptop without any trouble."

Despite all these incredible revelations, Alex remained firmly sceptical about what Alexander had told them.

"I just don't know about all this," he said. "I mean, Veronica only recently started working for her uncle. We'd never heard of her before. How could she have made all these plans in such a short time?"

"All you need to do is check into Veronica's background online," Alexander explained. "She's connected to many companies that will later work with her scheme, including a drone manufacturing company called Dominus. All you have to do is investigate all the news stories about her. They may seem innocent in your time, but they'll result in serious consequences in the future. Make sure you erase your search history when you've finished as well."

The message started to break up again.

"I'm sorry," said Alexander, "I'm losing the connection."

"So is Dad alive?" said Alex. "You must know what happened to him?"

But before Alexander could answer, the tablet's screen went blank. Alex tried several times to re-establish the connection but it was gone.

"Why wouldn't he tell me?" Alex said, in frustration.

"He might have been going to do that before the message broke up," replied Stephanie, with a shrug.

"He must know, if he's really who he says he is."

"Yes, and maybe you'll be able to ask him when, or if, he contacts us again, but you heard him about the connection. It's like us trying to connect to obsolete technology from the '70s or the '80s."

"I guess so," said Alex, still sounding very disappointed.

"Come on," said Stephanie, "let's order that pizza."

WHILE THEY WERE waiting for the pizza to arrive, they

used Stephanie's tablet to start their research into Veronica Castlewood's background. As Alexander had explained, there were a number of news stories and articles about Veronica and the people she'd been dealing with over the previous several years. The companies that she was most closely associated with were all involved with advanced technology or worked closely with such organizations. However, her business dealings all appeared to be perfectly legitimate. There was nothing that raised any red flags for Alex and Stephanie.

"Dominus UAV," said Stephanie, noting one of the news stories. "Didn't Alexander mention that company?"

"Yeah. Let's see what kind of work they do."

Stephanie connected to the company's website. Dominus were developing Unmanned Aerial Vehicles or UAVs. In the past, the company had conducted some work on drones for the military. Dominus had also worked with government bodies such as law enforcement agencies. They were currently focused on manufacturing a range of remote-controlled aircraft for commercial use. Their products were used by disaster relief organizations, surveying companies, wildlife protection agencies, movie producers, home delivery specialists, and surveillance and security companies. None of the company's projects seemed particularly sinister, but the various news stories and articles did confirm at least part of what Alexander had told them.

"Let's check out some of these other companies that she's been working with," said Stephanie, as she finished the last slice of pizza.

They worked until almost ten o'clock, learning as

much as they could about Veronica Castlewood and her activities.

"You should probably delete the browsing history," said Alex.

"Yeah, I'll do it in the morning."

"Well, don't forget," said Alex. "You usually leave that stuff on your tablet for months."

"Relax," said Stephanie, yawning. "I'll do it as soon as I get home. So do you think we should go over to Castlewood Dynamics?"

"We have to if we're going to get that laptop back," Alex reminded her.

"So we just walk right into her office and take it?"

"Alexander said she shouldn't be there tomorrow. Let's hope he's right."

They both heard a car in the driveway, followed by the sound of the car door closing.

"Mom's back," said Alex. "Better shut the tablet down."

As Angela walked toward the front door and turned in the key in the lock, Stephanie quickly closed all the websites they'd been studying. She didn't want Angela to catch a glimpse of what they'd been working on.

"Are you still here, Stephanie?" said Angela as she stepped into the sitting room. "Your mom's worried about you."

"Oh yeah," said Stephanie, pulling out her phone. "I put it on vibrate but haven't been checking the messages. Looks like she tried to call me twice."

"Yes, I know," said Angela, smiling. "She called me too. I told her I'd asked you to order pizza and that you two were probably wrapped up in something technical, as usual. Come on, I'll drive you home."

Stephanie sent her mom a quick text to apologize, grabbed her tablet then went to put on her shoes.

"See you tomorrow," said Alex, as Angela opened the front door and she and Stephanie stepped outside.

"Sure," said Stephanie. "I'll text you in the morning."

Chapter Seven
Castlewood Dynamics

ALEX SLEPT QUITE late the next day. It was just after 11 when the sound of a text alert woke him. At first, Alex thought it might be another message from Alexander, but the icon wasn't active. The text was from Stephanie. She was coming over in ten minutes. Alex got out of bed and had a quick shower before getting dressed. He staggered downstairs and went into the kitchen. He put a couple of slices of bread in the toaster. When they were ready, he quickly spread peanut butter on them. He'd just finished the second piece of toast when the doorbell rang. He went over and opened the door to find Stephanie standing on the doorstep.

"Sleep in?" he said, as he opened the door.

"Yeah," Stephanie replied, with a grin, "but so did you. Must be all that work we did researching those companies yesterday. Still, at least we can say it's still morning."

"Only just," said Alex, yawning.

Stephanie stepped inside and closed the door. Alex glanced at his phone. It was 11:25.

"Have you had any more messages from Alexander?"

"No, nothing. Maybe he'll get back to us after we've got the laptop?"

"True. After all, he should know when we get back here, shouldn't he? He seems to know everything else before we even do it. So how are we getting to Castlewood?"

"I guess we'll have to get a cab. Do you have any money?"

Stephanie pulled out her wallet and quickly scanned the contents.

"Not much. I've got $10 and some change."

"That's not going to be enough. I don't have any cash at all."

"So what are we going to do?"

"I don't know," said Alex, but then he had an idea. "Wait a minute. I could probably use my dad's credit card."

"Is that legal?"

"Technically no, but I know it's still active. The police told my mom to cancel the card, at least until we know what's happened to my dad, but she refused."

"Why did she do that?"

"She told me it was too much like giving up. To her it was kind of like accepting that he's not coming back."

"I can understand that," said Stephanie, nodding. "But won't we need to sign things, like the bill for the cab?"

"Don't worry," Alex assured her, with a wink. "Have you ever seen my dad's signature? I'll be right back."

He raced upstairs to Angela's room. His dad's wallet was on top of the dresser, along with a set of keys and some more of Andrew's belongings. Alex grabbed his dad's credit card from the wallet and hurried back downstairs.

"We shouldn't be too long over at Castlewood," he said. "I'll be able to put this back in the wallet well before Mom gets home."

"Wow," Stephanie said, studying the swirling scribble on the back of the card. "You weren't kidding about the signature."

"Told you," said Alex, as he keyed the taxi company's number into his phone. "I can easily forge that to fool anyone."

ON THE FORTY-five minute journey to Castlewood Dynamics, Alex and Stephanie discussed everything they'd learned so far. Alex still wasn't as convinced as Stephanie appeared to be about Alexander. However, Alex had decided that, as crazy as it seemed, Alexander might actually be on the level. They both agreed that they needed more information from Alexander but of course they had no way to contact him. Alexander had also mentioned that he'd had trouble establishing and maintaining a connection. They'd simply have to wait until they received another text or live message from him.

IT WAS JUST after 12:30 on Friday afternoon when they arrived at Castlewood Dynamics. Alex was nervous when he handed the cab driver his dad's credit card. Fortunately, the driver didn't ask any questions and barely glanced at the signature after Alex signed the receipt.

Castlewood Dynamics occupied a wide glass-fronted office complex in the heart of the area occupied by many corporate buildings in Silicon Valley. The company's silver logo was prominently displayed on the front of the building and on a large ornamental fountain in the centre of the spacious outer courtyard. It was the middle of the lunch hour for people working nearby, and men and women from the surrounding buildings were outside enjoying the summer sunshine. There were a number of people sitting around the fountain and others wandering in and out of the local restaurants and coffee shops. The sunlight shining on the glass-fronted surface of the Castlewood Dynamics building produced a blinding glare as Alex and Stephanie walked toward the building. The sliding doors parted and they walked into the lobby.

At the broad reception desk, a gleaming chrome company logo was attached to the front woodwork. A young woman with long dark hair cascading over her shoulders sat behind the desk. She occasionally looked over her glasses at her co-workers as they walked by, greeting them or simply smiling in their direction. She wore a headset and was simultaneously answering the phone as she feverishly tapped away at her computer keyboard. The woman immediately recognized Alex as he and Stephanie approached the desk.

"Well, hello," she said cheerily. "And what are you doing here?"

"Hi, Sandy," said Alex.

"And who's this?"

"This is my friend Stephanie."

"Is she as fond of taking things apart as you are?" said Sandy, with a smirk.

"Oh yeah," said Stephanie, laughing. "We do a lot of that kind of stuff together."

"I was so sorry to hear about your dad," said Sandy, changing her tone. "How are you and your mom doing?"

"Not bad," said Alex. "The police have been very good and keep us informed about what might have happened to him. We're not giving up hope."

"Is your mom okay? She didn't say much when she was here yesterday. She kept things to herself."

"She's doing fine," replied Alex. "Just coping really, not much else we can do."

"And Mr. Castlewood and his niece came over to the house," Stephanie said.

"Yes," said Sandy, nodding. "Your mom mentioned it when she was here yesterday, picking up a few things. Veronica's visiting Robert at the hospital."

"He's at the hospital?" asked Alex.

"But he seemed perfectly okay when we saw him," Stephanie added.

"He collapsed on the golf course," Sandy explained. "It's nothing serious as far as we know and they don't expect to keep him in for long. Working too hard, I suppose. I've told him he ought to start thinking about slowing down. So what are you two doing here? Oh, there goes the phone again. Castlewood Dynamics?"

While Sandy was talking on the phone, Alex and Stephanie observed the people passing through the lobby. Castlewood wasn't that big a corporation but had grown very quickly over the previous few years. They'd only moved into their current building around eighteen months earlier and were hiring more people all the time.

"So what did you say you needed?" said Sandy, as she finished her call.

"We need to collect my dad's laptop."

"Oh, didn't your mom get that yesterday with the other stuff?"

"Well, er," Alex started to say.

"She forgot," said Stephanie, thinking quickly. "It's in his office."

"Okay, well if you just want to go and get it," said Sandy. "You know where it is right, Alex?"

"I do."

"Okay, I'll open the door."

Sandy activated the switch on her desk. The glass door slid open so that Alex and Stephanie could access the Castlewood offices and laboratory areas.

"See you two in a bit. Hello, Castlewood Dynamics."

ONCE THEY WERE out of sight of the reception desk, Alex and Stephanie stopped to get their bearings.

"Did you hear what she said?" Stephanie asked. "Robert's in the hospital, just like Alexander said he would be."

"No, he said he was going to die," Alex corrected her. "Sandy said that Veronica's just visiting him there."

"But Alexander still predicted that it would happen."

"Yeah, I know. Let's hope he's not right about

everything then."

"So do you know where Veronica's office is?"

"No, but I know where Robert's is, so it might be close to there. This way."

THE OFFICES ALL looked very much the same to Stephanie. Alex had visited the company headquarters several times before and knew where he was going.

"That's Robert's," he said, as they approached a large office.

They paused for a moment and looked inside. There were a number of pictures on the walls, along with plaques and framed awards. A bronze sculpture presented to Robert by the local business community stood on the cluttered desk beside the phone. There was also a picture in a frame of Robert's late wife, beside his favourite Castlewood Dynamics coffee mug.

"That could be Veronica's office next door," said Alex. "Let's have a look."

The office beside Robert's was slightly smaller than his. The walls were devoid of decoration, and the entire office was clean and tidy, with nothing out of place. The desk had a computer, a phone, and a stack of plastic trays in which some papers, folders, and documents were neatly placed. Alex and Stephanie quickly scanned the office but there was no sign of Andrew's laptop.

"Maybe she took it with her to the hospital?" Stephanie suggested.

"That seems a little strange," said Alex. "Maybe she just didn't bring it to work and she's investigating the laptop's files at home?"

"That seems a little odd too though," Stephanie replied. "Didn't she say that they had to look over some official company material?"

"She did," agreed Alex. "But if she's looking for something else, she'd want to do that in private. And maybe she's tricking Robert anyway, so that he doesn't think there's anything wrong with what she's doing?"

"This is that drone company," Stephanie said, taking a colourful brochure from one of the desk's in-trays.

The Dominus brochure had a yellow post-it note attached. There was a scribbled message stating 10 am the following day. Veronica's desktop computer was turned off so they couldn't see what she'd recently been working on but there was clear evidence of her links to Dominus.

"It looks like Alexander was telling us the truth," said Stephanie.

"This only proves that she's working with the company or maybe just interested in talking to them. Remember, we never saw anything on their website that looked suspicious."

"True, but look at this."

Stephanie showed Alex a business card that she'd picked up from beside the phone. The card belonged to someone working at Hartfield Tech.

"Isn't this the company your dad was thinking of going to work for?"

"It is," Alex replied, frowning. "I wonder why she's been talking to them?"

"Maybe she knows about your dad's plans to leave the company?"

"You might be right, but . . ."

They both heard voices in the hallway outside the office. Alex and Stephanie ducked behind Veronica's desk as three Castlewood employees walked past the office door, deeply engaged in conversation. Alex and Stephanie remained hidden until the people had safely passed by.

"I think they've gone," said Stephanie, peering over the top of the desk.

"That was too close," said Alex, as he got to his feet. "Let's get out of here. We can't get the laptop anyway."

They hurried back to the front desk, where Sandy was still busy at her keyboard and occasionally answering the phone.

"Did you find what you were looking for?" she asked, as Alex and Stephanie stood beside the desk.

Before they could answer Sandy's phone rang again.

"Castlewood Dynamics. Yes, this is Sandy."

Suddenly her face drained of colour.

"Yes, yes," she said, her voice trembling. "I'll let everyone know. Thank you, Veronica."

"What is it?" Alex asked.

"What's wrong?" said Stephanie.

"It's Mr. Castlewood," said Sandy, struggling to speak. "He's passed away."

She removed her glasses as her deep brown eyes began to fill with tears.

"I'm sorry," she muttered. "I have to let everyone know."

She stood up from her chair and disappeared through the sliding doors into the Castlewood Dynamics offices. Alex and Stephanie looked at the clock on the wall behind the reception desk. It was 1 pm.

Alex and Stephanie hurried outside and quickly called another cab. He and Stephanie didn't talk much on the homeward journey. They were both trying to process everything that had just happened. They also didn't want the driver to overhear them and perhaps wonder what was going on. Alex and Stephanie both realized that they needed to talk to Alexander. Unfortunately, they had no idea when he would next be in contact.

WHEN THEY ARRIVED back at Alex's house, he received a message just as the cab drove away. While he and Stephanie stood on the sidewalk, Alex took out his phone. It was Alexander. Pressing the icon, the video opened although it was very distorted.

"Sorry," said Alexander. "I'm having trouble establishing a connection. I guess you've just got back from Castlewood? So do you believe me now? Robert's dead, isn't he?"

"Yes," Alex replied. "It looks that way."

"But he was so healthy," said Stephanie.

"Yes, he was," Alexander agreed. "And now Veronica has control of the company. The police will investigate Robert's sudden death. That's all standard procedure, but the poison Veronica used is impossible to detect or to ever trace back to her."

"Poison?" said Alex, in astonishment.

Before Alexander could elaborate, the video transmission on the phone began to break up.

"I might lose the connection at any time," said Alexander. "Do you have the laptop?"

"No," replied Alex.

"It wasn't there," Stephanie added.

"What do you mean?" said Alexander. "It had to be."

"We couldn't find it in her office," Stephanie replied. "Maybe she took it with her to the hospital?"

"I don't understand," said Alexander. "The laptop was supposed to be there."

By now his image was barely visible on the phone's screen.

"I have to go," said Alexander. "One last thing, Alex. Your mom has some news for you."

"What about?" Alex asked.

But Alexander was gone.

ALEX AND STEPHANIE walked up the path toward the house. To Alex's surprise, his mom's car was in the garage. He figured that she must have come home early from work. As he and Stephanie stepped into the house, Angela was sitting at the kitchen table. She quickly straightened her long brown hair as they approached. She looked as if she'd been crying.

"What's wrong, Mom?" said Alex. "Are you okay?"

"Hi Alex, Stephanie. Please sit down. I have something to tell you."

Chapter Eight
Revelations

ALEX AND STEPHANIE sat down at the kitchen table.

"I'm afraid I have some bad news," said Angela. "Robert Castlewood is dead."

"What?" said Alex, pretending to be surprised.

"Oh no," said Stephanie, following his lead. "What happened?"

"It was at the golf course earlier today. He just collapsed and had to be rushed to hospital. It seemed okay at first. He didn't seem to be in any danger at all but then he died."

Angela was struggling to hold back her tears.

"Sandy called me on my cell phone at lunchtime when I was in the car. I decided not to go back to work and to come straight home. I thought you'd need to know right away. Robert's been so good to us since the accident."

"But he was going to do that half-marathon, wasn't he?" said Alex.

"Yeah," said Stephanie. "Wasn't he supposed to be very fit for his age?"

"Yes, I believe so," said Angela, "but I guess we never know when it's our time. There's something else too. It's about Dad."

"What about him?"

Angela paused and took a deep breath before continuing.

"I was speaking with the police earlier today. Officer Marino thinks at some point we may have to come to terms with the fact that your dad may be dead."

She reached over and touched Alex's hand.

"No," said Alex, pulling his hand away, scarcely believing what he was hearing. "No, this can't be happening."

"I'm sorry, Alex. I just wanted you to be prepared for the worst. To be honest, I'm not sure if I could ever accept it, especially since they still haven't found a body or anything. I need to go and talk to the police officers at the station and learn more in person. I wanted to tell you both myself though, before I left. Are you going to be okay?"

"Yeah, sure," said Alex, although he really wasn't feeling very good at all. "I'm fine, honestly."

"Okay," said Angela, although her expression indicated that she wasn't entirely convinced. "I won't be too long at the police station. Can you stay here until I get back, Stephanie?"

"Yes, of course, no problem," Stephanie replied.

Angela stood up from the kitchen table. She was clearly holding back her tears as she gave Alex a peck on the cheek before quickly leaving.

"ARE YOU OKAY?" said Stephanie, once the front door had closed.

"Yeah, I'm fine."

Alex felt as if a million thoughts were running back and forth in his mind. His stomach was also churning at the thought that his dad might really be dead.

"Really?" said Stephanie. "I'm so sorry to hear about your dad."

"It's not true," Alex shot back. "You heard what my mom said. I mean, Dad could still be alive and ..."

They were both startled by an alert from Alex's phone. Alexander had sent another text message. Alex quickly opened it.

I'm going to try and connect to the wifi in the house and communicate with you through the TV. Turn it to Channel 3 please.

Alex and Stephanie left the kitchen table and went into the sitting room. Stephanie picked up the remote and activated the TV. She and Alex watched in amazement as an image of Alexander flickered into view on the screen.

"Can you see me okay?" he asked.

The room behind him was filled with a bewildering array of scientific equipment in varying states of repair, including computers, monitors, and some gadgets that neither Alex nor Stephanie immediately recognized.

"Yes," said Stephanie. "It's very sharp this time."

"Is it true about Dad?" asked Alex.

"Ah yes," Alexander replied. "Your mom just told you about what the police suggested, didn't she? I remember that so well."

"Is it true?" Alex repeated. "Is he dead? I mean,

will he be declared dead?"

"I'm afraid so. I didn't want to tell you until the time was right."

"Alex, I'm so sorry," said Stephanie, placing her hand on his arm.

"So he's really gone?" Alex asked.

"Yes. I recall that chat with Mom when I got back from Castlewood. It was tough to learn about Robert and Dad in the same day. If it's any consolation, Alex, I really do know how you feel."

"Yes, I suppose you do," said Alex.

He was still trying to fully comprehend the insanity of what was happening. Alexander cleared his throat before continuing.

"It all seems so long ago now," he said. "And now so much has changed since then. Mom refused to accept that he was dead, despite the official verdict, since no body was ever found. She kept the cause alive for years but then eventually died quite unexpectedly."

"She's going to die soon too?" Alex asked, beginning to panic.

"Not soon, it'll be a while yet," Alexander reassured him. "It was very sudden though, and I've always suspected that she died from the same poison that killed Robert Castlewood."

"She's going to be murdered?" said Alex, his voice shaking.

"Veronica only had patience for so long. Mom's insistence that there was a suspicious unsolved disappearance kept the story about Dad in the public eye. Mom never had any prospect of finding any evidence to support her claims that Dad had been kidnapped and might even still be alive. She also couldn't hope to prove that he'd possibly been killed and buried somewhere secretly. Veronica eventually decided to silence her. At least, that's my opinion."

Alex didn't know what to say anymore. He simply sat on the couch in stunned silence.

"What about me?" asked Stephanie. "Can you tell me what happens to me?"

"I shouldn't really reveal anything about your future, Stephanie," Alexander replied.

"Why not?" said Alex. "You've told us so much already. If you're worried about us knowing things that'll affect our future, you've left it a little late."

"I suppose that's true," said Alexander, with a sigh.

"So what happens to me in the future?" Stephanie asked again.

Alexander swallowed hard and paused before replying.

"I lost touch with you and your family once we'd both grown up. I didn't see you again after I reached my early twenties, but I do know that here in the future, you and your family are dead."

"Oh, my God," Stephanie gasped. "All of us?"

"I'm afraid so," said Alexander.

"Were they murdered too?" Alex asked.

"I'm not sure," admitted Alexander. "It's a possibility that they were killed because of their connection to my family but I don't know for certain. So many have died since Veronica began her mission."

"So you mentioned that recent events in our time set all this in motion," Stephanie said.

"Can you tell us what's going to happen?" asked Alex.

"Yes," Alexander replied. "In fact, you need to know as much as possible if we're to have any chance of stopping her. After Veronica poisoned her uncle, she took over the company and used Dad's research for her own sinister purposes. I never discovered the truth, but assume that Veronica arranged Dad's kidnapping to get him to reveal information he'd been holding back."

"About what?"

"I think he'd been getting suspicious of her motives. He'd decided to leave for Hartfield Tech and take his research work there with him."

"That business card that was on her desk for the other company," Stephanie said.

"That's right," agreed Alex. "She must have known what Dad was planning to do."

"Yes, I think so," Alexander confirmed. "The details about Dad's disappearance are very murky. However, he did have some crucial material on his laptop. Once Veronica accessed that she made her move. The robotic technology that had previously been developed in the Castlewood labs was subtly altered. Castlewood Dynamics steadily cornered the market in civilian robotics. They originally worked very closely with Dominus, but Castlewood soon completely absorbed them. Eventually all the world's other major companies such as Google, Apple, Microsoft, and many others were taken over directly or came to be controlled by Veronica's subsidiaries."

"Wow," said Stephanie. "So she controls just about everything?"

"In my time," Alexander replied, "Castlewood Dynamics doesn't exactly rule the world, but the company is far more powerful than most national governments."

"You mentioned something before about robots in your time," said Alex.

"Robots swiftly took over many of the world's menial tasks," Alexander continued. "In theory that's a great idea, but in practice it also put tens of millions of people out of work. This soon created severe social problems but Veronica and her company solved this. In my time, people who are no longer useful are simply eliminated."

"Eliminated?" said Stephanie.

"Robots now do most of the work, serving an extremely wealthy elite," Alexander replied. "Those unable to contribute to society are simply rounded up and killed, as are dissenters. People are easily identified and arrested since all the planet's technology is so connected these days. Population numbers are also tightly controlled in order to conserve the world's dwindling natural resources."

"How do we know you're telling us the truth?" asked Alex.

"You don't," Alexander admitted. "I know how hard this is to believe, but perhaps I can show you."

Chapter Nine
The Shape of Things To Come

ALEXANDER TYPED SOMETHING into the keyboard of his computer.

"Keep watching the screen," he said. "I'm going to show you the future."

His image vanished from the TV and was replaced by scenes from a busy city. The bustling sidewalks were filled with people, and the streets were congested with traffic. According to some of the surrounding buildings and subway signs, it appeared to be New York City. The streets and buildings looked much the same as they did in the present, but Alex and Stephanie agreed that there were a few subtle differences. Some of the names of the stores and restaurants looked familiar, while others didn't. The cars and other vehicles looked similar to what Alex and Stephanie were used to, although there were some futuristic designs. They noticed that some of the fashions in the future resembled ones from their own time while others were different or appeared to be a combination of old and new styles of dress.

"As you can see," said Alexander, providing a voiceover, "the world hasn't changed that much. After all, it's only been thirty years. Things changed quite dramatically at the turn of the century with the advent of the Internet and everything else related to computers. The pace of technological change seemed to be getting faster every year back then. However, once Veronica tightened her grip on everything, technological innovation was all in the hands of one group of people. Developments that could be of real benefit to the general public were few and far between."

The screen then altered to reveal a closer view of the people walking up and down the street. Alex and Stephanie were astounded as holographic images of objects or talking people abruptly appeared on the sidewalk out of thin air. Most people walked straight through the images that then simply disappeared. Sometimes the images remained in place and continued talking to the next passing pedestrian.

"I guess this is the equivalent of TV or radio advertising in your time," said Alexander. "The holographic images are everywhere, trying to sell people things. They're all tailored to a person's tastes and previous buying history. Phones and all the other networks are all interconnected. If a company knows you purchased something once, they pursue you relentlessly."

"How can people stand that?" said Stephanie.

Alexander simply shrugged.

"I guess they get used to it."

On the TV screen, four objects came into view in the sky above the street. As the objects drew closer, Alex and Stephanie could see that they were small grey aircraft, around the size of gaming consoles. They appeared to be equipped with a number of retractable devices on each side, along with lights in a range of colours. The aircraft also had legs tucked underneath them. They had no rotors and the objects just seemed to glide silently and effortlessly through the air. As they hovered above the street, each one emitted a pale blue beam. This was slowly shone up and down random individuals as they moved along the sidewalk. The pedestrians appeared unfazed by this and simply continued on their way as if nothing had happened. The aircraft then hovered for a few seconds above the street before zooming away at high speed and disappearing into the sky.

The city scene then vanished and the view on the TV resumed showing Alexander.

"What were those?" said Alex.

"Drones," Alexander replied. "Developed by Dominus and based at least partially on designs by Castlewood Dynamics, including Dad's ideas."

"What were they doing?" asked Stephanie.

"Scanning people. The drones can learn everything about someone with those beams. Physical, financial, legal, medical, you name it."

"What for?" said Alex.

"Were they looking for criminals or something?" Stephanie asked.

"No, probably just a routine scan," Alexander explained. "These days the population's so tightly controlled. It's very easy for the authorities to make someone just disappear so everyone's learned to try and stay out of trouble. Some of the drones are armed with energy beam weapons. The ones you saw are just the patrolling models but they can easily call for back up from their more lethal counterparts, if needed."

"Why would they do that?" said Alex.

"Despite all the restrictions on society, there are still some dissenters, but they don't last long. Unless they're like me and can stay one step away from the law."

"What do you mean?" Stephanie asked.

"I have lots of ways to stay hidden," said Alexander. "But even I have to go out sometimes to get food and other supplies. I have to make sure that I don't get scanned by one of the drones."

"How do you do that if they're always checking up on people at random?" Alex asked.

"With this," replied Alexander.

He held up slim, chrome-coloured metal bracelet. It had three very small buttons set closely together.

"This is a mobile molecular scrambler."

"A what?" said Stephanie.

"I program it here before I go out," Alexander began. "It scrambles my molecular pattern, my signal, if you like, so that the drones can't read it. If they get too close, I can also confuse the drones by mixing my pattern with that of someone nearby. This means that the drones never scan me. If they did, I'd soon be arrested. They've been looking for me for years."

"Can you show us more?" Alex asked.

"No, that's enough for now," said Alexander. "I just wanted to give you some assurances that I was telling the truth. As I said, I can accept that this is very hard for you to believe. So you're sure the laptop wasn't there in Veronica's office?"

"No, we couldn't find it," replied Alex.

"I still don't understand that," Alexander said, frowning. "It was supposed to be there. All I can think of is that my instructions to you are making subtle alterations to the timeline in your era. I'm not sure why that would have affected Veronica not leaving the laptop at Castlewood though. Changes in your time will also make things more unpredictable for me here in the future."

"Is that bad?" asked Stephanie.

"No idea," Alexander confessed. "I've never done this before."

NONE OF THEM heard Angela's car arrive. They were all startled at the sound of her key opening the front door.

"I'll contact you again in the morning," said Alexander.

His image disappeared from the TV screen and was replaced by a car commercial.

"Hi," said Angela as she walked into the sitting room. "Who were you talking to?"

"No one," said Alex.

"I thought I heard somebody's voice," said Angela.

"Oh that," Stephanie replied. "It was just an interactive game on the computer, that's all."

"What did the police say?" asked Alex, quickly changing the subject.

"Not too much actually," Angela replied. "They just repeated what they said before. You know, about declaring your dad to be officially dead, but I'm just not sure if I want that to happen."

She frowned as she gently massaged the bridge of her nose.

"I'll tell you more about it later. I'm getting a really bad migraine and need to lie down for a hour or so."

"Okay," said Alex.

"Bye," said Stephanie.

Angela smiled at them before turning to head upstairs.

"SHAME WE CAN'T talk to Alexander again now," said Alex, once Angela had closed her bedroom door. "I guess we'll just have to wait until tomorrow. Maybe by then he'll have worked out why we couldn't find the laptop."

"I guess," said Stephanie, with a shrug.

"What's wrong?"

"I just don't know about all this, Alex," she replied. "I mean, how do we know we should really be listening to him?"

"Wait a second. I thought I was the one who doubted him? You've been telling me that we have to go along with this."

"I know, I know," she said. "But we still haven't see any real evidence that he's telling the truth."

"But he knows about things before they happen. How else could he do that if he's not from the future?"

"I don't know," Stephanie snapped, in frustration. "Maybe he really is on the level, but I still don't know if we should trust him."

"And what about those scenes from the future that he showed us?"

"I've been thinking about that. If he really is from the future, he's admitted that he has access to advanced technology. All that could have been faked."

"But why would he do that?"

Stephanie paused before continuing.

"What if he's not trying to stop Veronica at all?"

"What do you mean?"

"What if he's actually working for her in the future? What if everything he's telling us is just designed to get us to do things that will help Veronica's plans come true?"

"Hold on a second," said Alex. "This is weird enough as it is. So you think he's just giving us false information on purpose?"

"I'm not sure," she replied. "And this thing about him not knowing where the laptop is got me thinking. He'd have to know about that, surely, if he's really trying to help us."

"I suppose so, but . . ."

"And if he's part of an evil empire in the future, he's at least partly responsible for killing millions of people, including my parents and your mom. If we do nothing to help him, that future won't happen."

"But we don't know that for certain either," Alex protested.

"I'm sorry, Alex," said Stephanie, firmly, as she stood up from the couch. "I've made up my mind. I don't know much about Veronica. I have no idea what her plans might be, but I don't think we should get involved."

"But we're already involved," Alex insisted. "Are you saying that we should just forget about all this?"

"Yes, we should."

"And what about my dad? Are we supposed to just forget about him too? Alexander can help him."

"How do you know that for sure? We have no idea if he's telling the truth."

"But what about all the things he knows? The things he showed us about the future?"

"We don't know how real any of that is, Alex. I just don't trust him."

"And then . . ."

"Look," Stephanie interrupted. "I don't want to discuss this anymore, okay?"

She hurried over to the front door, but Alex followed her.

"But, Stephanie," Alex pleaded, as she slipped on her shoes. "This is crazy. You can't mean this."

She didn't say another word and simply opened the front door before running off into the night without a backward glance.

Chapter Ten
Expect The Unexpected

ALEX SENT STEPHANIE several texts that evening but received no response. He could only hope that she would feel a little better about everything the next day. He spent a fair amount of time wondering if she was right about him becoming something he currently wasn't. Yet, it was so difficult to make any sense of it all. It was certainly possible that Alexander might be leading them astray. Perhaps he also wasn't really who he said he was, but it was all so hard to fathom.

The remainder of Alex's evening involved researching the websites about Veronica's past and her business dealings. He wanted to see if he could spot anything he'd missed when he and Stephanie had looked at the sites earlier, but still, nothing in particular stood out. He was surprised when his mom came downstairs to get a glass of water from the kitchen.

"Hey, Alex," she said, as she stepped into the sitting room. "What are you still doing up?"

"Nothing much," he replied, as he promptly closed the laptop screen.

"What are you doing?"

"Just a new game I found the other day. I've had enough of it for now, to be honest."

"When did Stephanie leave?"

"A while ago. She said she had to be home earlier than usual tonight."

"Okay," said Angela, nodding. "How's she doing? I spoke to her mom and dad the other day and they said that Stephanie's recovered very well from the accident."

"Yeah," Alex replied. "She seems to be doing okay. At least she doesn't have a scar on her forehead."

They both laughed.

"That's true," said Angela, smiling.

She sat down at the other end of the couch and placed her glass of water on the coffee table.

"And how about you?"

"Me? I'm fine."

Angela reached across and gently squeezed his hand.

"I hope so, Alex. I know this hasn't been easy for you, for either of us. I'm sorry I've not been around much after work and at the weekends, I've just had so much to do with the police and the lawyers and everything else."

"It's okay, Mom," Alex assured her. "I know what you've had to do. I just wish I could help you with some of it."

"That's very sweet, Alex, thank you."

"And I'm sure they'll find Dad soon."

Angela smiled but was clearly fighting to hold back her tears. She took a sip from her water.

"Yes," she agreed. "I'm sure they will too. Something will probably turn up soon. As you know, the police have been very helpful and kind. I've been dealing quite often with the two officers who came to see you at the hospital. I've mostly spoken with Officer Marino. Do you remember her?"

"Yeah," Alex replied. "She seemed very nice."

Angela smiled again and gave Alex's hand another gentle squeeze.

"Okay, I'd better go back to bed. I have another hectic day tomorrow."

She stood up and grabbed her glass of water from the coffee table.

"Don't stay up too late."

"I won't. Night, Mom."

"Goodnight, Alex."

She turned and left the sitting room then headed up the stairs. Once Alex heard her bedroom door close, he reopened the laptop. When the screen reactivated, it still displayed the website belonging to one of the companies that he and Stephanie had been researching earlier. Alex contemplated doing some more work looking into Veronica's business dealings but accepted that it was time to call it a night. With a yawn, he closed the web page then signed out of his email.

He thought about Stephanie as he waited for the laptop to shut down. He quickly checked his phone even though he knew that she hadn't been trying to message him. All he could do was try texting Stephanie again in the morning and hope that she was in a better mood. The laptop finally shut down so he closed the screen and carried the computer up to his room.

SURPRISINGLY, ALEX WAS able to sleep well, despite going to bed with his mind still racing. Angela had gone out by the time that Alex woke up at 11:30 on Saturday morning. To his disappointment, there were no messages from Stephanie. He figured she must still be mad at him, but decided he'd go over to her house to see if he could reason with her. Perhaps sleeping on it had mellowed her attitude? Alternatively, maybe he and Stephanie could at least talk about her misgivings concerning Alexander and the bizarre situation they found themselves in.

Alex immediately noticed the three police cars as he turned the corner into Stephanie's street. The vehicles were parked outside Stephanie's house and there were several uniformed officers standing on the front lawn. Some of them were talking to Stephanie's parents. Alex quickened his pace as he approached the house. The front door was wide open and he could see that there was some damage inside. Two of the windows were also broken. As Alex arrived at the house, one of the police officers turned to greet him. It was Officer Marino, whom he'd spoken to at the hospital.

"Hi, Alex," she said, smiling. "I thought I recognized you. How are you feeling? Looks like the accident left quite a scar on your forehead."

"I'm fine, thanks," said Alex. "What's going on here?"

Stephanie's parents were deep in conversation with the other officers in front of the house. Stephanie's mother looked very upset as she answered the officers' questions.

"There's been a break in," replied Marino. "No one's been hurt, but your friend's missing."

"Stephanie?" said Alex.

"Yes, you've saved me a trip, actually. I was going to come over and see you later today."

"What's happened? What do you mean she's missing?"

"There was a break in earlier today, probably just after Mr. and Mrs. Thomas left the house. We think Stephanie was still sleeping. There was some damage to the house. Some windows were broken and a few drawers had been opened, as if the crooks were looking for something, but apparently nothing of value was taken. However, Stephanie's now missing, along with her tablet. There were a couple of other laptops in the house but they weren't touched. There's no ransom note or anything like that, which we'd expect if she'd been kidnapped. Her parents haven't had any messages either. Right now, we don't have any leads, although the guys are still going through the house to see if there's any evidence we can follow up on."

Alex froze. Had Stephanie been kidnapped just like his dad might have been? He tried to maintain a poker face as he listened to Officer Marino.

"When did you last see her?"

"She was over at my house last night. We were just hanging out."

"Was your mom at home too?"

"Yes, but she went to bed early. She wasn't feeling well. I guess the stress has been getting to her lately, with everything that's happened."

"What time did Stephanie go home?"

"Early evening. I'm sorry, I don't remember the exact time."

"Did she say she was going straight home?"

"As far as I know. She never mentioned that she was going to be doing something else. I assume she just went home for dinner."

Marino nodded.

"And you didn't text each other or anything else last night?"

"No, nothing like that. We don't always chat online or message each other if we've already spent most of the day together."

Alex declined to mention that he and Stephanie had had an argument. He also didn't tell Marino that Stephanie hadn't been answering his texts the previous evening or that morning.

"What did you do in the daytime?" asked Marino.

Alex hesitated. Did Marino know he and Stephanie had been to Castlewood Dynamics? How could she have found out about that?

"Same thing, really," he replied. "Just hanging out playing games and stuff most of the time."

"You didn't go out at all? It was such nice day yesterday."

"Yeah, I know, but we decided to stay in. Is it important what we did?"

"Just trying to get a clear picture, Alex," Marino replied, smiling. "You never know what might be helpful. If you think of anything, give me a call. You still have my card, right?"

"Yes," said Alex. "I hope she's okay."

"So do we, Alex. Will you be home later? We might want to talk to you and your mom about what's happened."

"What for?" asked Alex, trying not to panic.

He certainly didn't want the police poking around at his home or taking an interest in his phone or his laptop. He also wanted to avoid them looking at messages from the mysterious Alexander, even if they weren't genuine.

"Just routine," Marino replied. "Apart from Stephanie's parents, you and your mom were probably the last people that saw her. We need to follow up on everything, I'm sure you understand."

"Yes, of course," said Alex, trying to remain calm.

"Anyway," said Marino. "I'd better go back and talk to her parents. Thanks again."

She smiled before turning to rejoin the other officers.

ALEX CALMLY WALKED to the end of Stephanie's street. Once he turned the corner he quickened his pace and hurried home, his mind in a whirl. He didn't want to believe it but it seemed as if Veronica might have captured Stephanie. And if Veronica had the tablet, she'd also know all about what he and Stephanie had been investigating. Even if she didn't know anything about the reasons for the research, Veronica would probably still be suspicious regarding why they'd been looking into both her past and present business dealings. She might even be aware that they were at the company offices the previous day. Alex started to panic when he realized that some of Alex's messages had been communicated through the tablet. If Veronica had that in her possession, she'd know about Alexander as well. Alex stopped walking when he felt his phone vibrate. He took it out of his pocket and saw that

Alexander was trying to contact him. Alex sat on a bench at a bus stop to access the message. Before Alexander could say anything, Alex told him what had happened and that Stephanie was missing.

"What do you mean missing?" asked Alexander. "That's not supposed to happen."

"What are you talking about? I thought you knew how things were going to happen here in our time. Hasn't this all happened before, as far as you're concerned?"

"Yes. I mean, I don't know. This is all very confusing."

"Veronica's probably kidnapped Stephanie," said Alex. "If she's got Stephanie's tablet, it'll show all the research we were doing about her."

"Yes," Alexander agreed, "but that won't prove anything."

"We also talked to you on the tablet, remember?" Alex pointed out. "Unless Stephanie deleted the history, that's going to show up on there as well."

Alexander thought for a moment before answering, furrowing his brow.

"Okay, let's try not to panic. We don't know—"

"She could even be hurt or worse," said Alex, interrupting him. "My dad might be dead and Veronica poisoned Robert as well. You know what she's capable of. How could you not know about all this?"

"I don't know, Alex. This didn't occur before. Like I already told you, your actions based on the information I'm giving you must be altering the timeline somehow but it's just a theory."

Alex wasn't convinced.

"Or maybe you're not telling me everything," he

said. "Are you holding stuff back?"

A few people walking by the bus stop glanced over as Alex's anger mounted and he raised his voice while using the phone. Yet Alex was beyond caring. As far as he was concerned, Alexander wasn't being straight with him.

"Where's Stephanie?" Alex demanded.

"I can understand your confusion," replied Alexander, "but let's try and look at this logically. I agree that Veronica might have taken Stephanie, but I have no idea where she is. Like I told you, this never happened before. I remember back then that Veronica operated several different facilities in other buildings apart from the main Castlewood complex but I don't recall the exact locations."

"I don't believe you," said Alex. "You have to know. Why won't you tell me? Stephanie could be in real danger."

"Sorry, Alex, I don't know what to tell you. I'll do my best to investigate these events. I don't know when I'll be able to be in contact again. All my computers here are designed to avoid being tracked, and it's vital that I'm not discovered. I usually move locations on a regular basis to avoid detection by the authorities."

The video message began to break up.

"I've also faked details of my own death many times and changed identities frequently. However, I've been forced to stay at this apartment for longer than I usually like. I needed to get all the right equipment so that I could contact you in the past, but it's becoming too dangerous to maintain this link."

Before Alex could ask him any more questions, Alexander was gone.

Chapter Eleven
The Mansion

ON HIS WAY back home, Alex began to second-guess himself. He wondered about what Stephanie had said about Alexander. Was it true that there was something just not right, and at times downright suspicious, about the entire situation? Alex admitted that it was uncanny that Alexander knew so much about the course of events. He'd more or less convinced himself that Alexander really was from the future. Yet why was there such a discrepancy in what he knew about events, especially something as important as Stephanie's disappearance? Surely he would have known about that? Then there was the situation with the laptop too.

Alex didn't buy the theory Alexander had put forward about the timeline changing because he was guiding Alex and Stephanie. Okay, he accepted that the situation was very weird but the theory still didn't ring true. Maybe Stephanie was right? Perhaps Alex couldn't trust his future self after all? And what if all the recent events were actually the cause of Alex becoming Alexander? If his future self really was evil and in league with Veronica, could Alex even stop things? Maybe even doubting Alexander's sincerity and second guessing himself was all somehow part of how things were supposed to happen? Or maybe events couldn't be changed anyway and everything was inevitable, no matter what Alex did in his own time. It was maddeningly confusing.

Alex then had an idea. Both he and Stephanie had apps on their phones that could track each other's locations. He wondered if he could learn where she was, presuming she still had her phone with her. Alex sat down on the bench at another bus stop. He activated the app and saw that Stephanie had been at home earlier in the day. Her phone also indicated that she'd then been closer to one of the area's more upscale neighbourhoods before the signal stopped. Alex conceded that someone could have stolen Stephanie's phone and that could be the source of the trace signal. However, it was the only lead he had related to Stephanie's possible location. And based on what had happened to his dad and then to Robert, Alex was convinced that Stephanie was in terrible danger.

HE WAS ABOUT to put his phone back in his pocket and go home when there was another video message from Alexander. Alex reluctantly opened the message, which was marred by static.

"What do you want?" said Alex.

"Look, I know you're suspicious, Alex, but don't go home. Please."

"Why not? I thought you couldn't predict what was going to happen anymore? Lost your magic powers?"

Alexander ignored the question.

"I don't know what's happened to Stephanie, but if she's been kidnapped, whoever took her might also be targeting you. The police are obviously still in your area, but once they've gone, maybe tonight or when your mom's gone to work, you could be next."

"What do you suggest?" asked Alex.

"You need to get Dad's laptop."

"But we don't know where it is."

"It's at the Castlewood mansion."

"How do you know that?" Alex demanded, angrily. "I thought everything was all screwed up now? And why should I trust you anyway?"

"I know this is hard, Alex. I know you have doubts but the laptop is there, believe me. You know where the mansion is, right?"

"Yes, I went there with Dad a couple of times."

"Veronica won't be there. I know that she went to New York right after Robert's death to deal with lawyers and then to sign the government deal in Washington. Veronica has an office in the mansion. It used to be Robert's and should be easy enough to find."

"Yes, I think I remember where Robert's office was."

The video screen became consumed with static, although Alex could still hear the audio reasonably clearly.

"Good, you should be fine then. If you don't believe me about Veronica being away, just check on one of the local news websites. There'll be something about it since she's in the news in your time right now. Check it out and . . ."

Then he was gone, yet again.

IT WAS SO frustrating that Alexander only revealed a portion of the story. Whether this was a genuine issue caused by him connecting from the future or just a ruse, Alex just couldn't tell anymore.

He did, however, decide to take Alexander's advice and use his phone to check the local news channels online. Sure enough, there was coverage of Veronica, including a few pictures and a video of her at the airport. She was with a man who was fielding questions from reporters. Veronica was apparently headed to New York and Washington on business and wasn't expected to be back in town for several days.

When Alex noticed the map showing the location of the airport on the website, he suddenly realized the possible significance of what he'd seen on his phone earlier. Stephanie, or at least her phone, had been in the part of the city where the Castlewood mansion was located. Was it possible that she'd been taken there? It would make sense if Veronica had instructed her people to take Stephanie somewhere secure, rather than to the company headquarters. The mansion was as large as four or five regular houses and had many rooms. There were also stables and other buildings within the extensive grounds. There were plenty of places where Stephanie could easily be held prisoner. If he followed Alexander's instructions and went to the mansion to get the laptop, Alex might be able to rescue Stephanie too. This also gave Alex new hope that he could perhaps change things after all. Rescuing Stephanie was his own idea, not something that had originated with Alexander. Maybe his fate wasn't carved in stone after all?

ALEX DECIDED NOT to go home, at least not until his mom returned. If she was around and her car was on the driveway, it might deter someone from snatching him. Stephanie had apparently been at home alone when she'd disappeared. Alex brought up the map location of the mansion on his phone. It wasn't that far away but he needed to get there quickly. He still had Andrew's credit card in his wallet so he quickly called a cab.

He didn't have to wait too long before the car arrived.

"Where can I drop you?" asked the driver, as Alex slid into the back seat.

"This is the address," he replied.

He leaned forward and showed the map on his phone to the driver. He quickly scanned the map and nodded.

"Sure, no problem."

Alex eased back into his seat and fastened his seat belt as the cab pulled away.

The twenty-minute journey was undertaken mostly in silence. Alex was relieved that the cab driver wasn't too chatty. Alex desperately needed to be able to think and attempt to process everything that was running through his mind, however complex it was. Alex also tried to formulate some kind of plan regarding how he'd proceed once he arrived at his destination. And yet as the cab approached the imposing iron gates at the front of the Castlewood mansion, Alex still had no idea what he was going to do.

"Here we are," said the driver, as he slowed down.

"Can you stop just a little further along the street?" Alex asked.

"Okay," replied the driver.

He drove just beyond the gates and stopped.

"That's great, thanks," said Alex, handing the driver the credit card.

Once the payment was processed, Alex climbed out of the cab. He watched it drive away before walking back to the iron gates. They stood at the end of a short curved driveway that led up to the front of the mansion. Alex was relieved that there wasn't a camera mounted anywhere near the gate, or at least not one that he could see. He knew that a high-tech company like Castlewood Dynamics could have hidden cameras situated just about anywhere but he also knew that he had to take the risk. If he was right about Stephanie being held prisoner here, he knew that he had to find her before Veronica returned from New York.

Although there were no obvious cameras, there was a security pad on the wall that presumably opened the gate. Alex figured that people probably scanned it from their cars as they approached. The gate was far too high for Alex climb over, as was the adjoining concrete wall. Yet Alex had hacked so many electronic devices over the years that he'd lost count. He prized open the cover of the security pad and carefully examined the circuit board. It was a fairly simple design. Alex accessed the code in less than a minute and the heavy gates swung open.

Alex quickly slipped inside, suspecting that the

gate would swing shut once he'd gone through. The gate closed just as a man emerged from the front door of the huge house to tend to the flowers and lawns. Alex darted behind one of the tall shrubs beside the gate. He watched as the gardener watered a few of the plants before activating the sprinkler system. The gardener then walked back to the corner of the house before turning toward the rear of the building. Alex couldn't see the stables and other structures that were at the rear of the house, but didn't notice any more of Veronica's people in the vicinity. He realized that there could be security guards present but Alex knew he had to take the risk. He ran across the lawn and up the driveway toward the front door, which the gardener had left ajar.

Alex cautiously opened the door and was relieved to see that there was no one around. The entrance hall had a marble floor and a high ceiling, from which a huge crystal chandelier was suspended. A winding staircase, also in marble, swept up to the second floor of the house where Robert's office was located. There were portraits of members of the Castlewood family on the walls of the entrance hall, along with several other paintings. Two decorative reproduction suits of armour stood at the foot of the staircase.

Alex crept across the hallway and was about to race up the staircase when he heard footsteps. He darted behind one of the suits of armour and held his breath. A woman emerged from the kitchen and walked across the entrance hall toward the front door. She was carrying a light jacket and had a set of keys in her hand. Alex figured the woman must have been leaving for the day after her shift in the kitchen. As soon as she stepped outside and closed the door behind her, Alex emerged from his hiding place. That had been close, he thought, his heart racing. He wondered how many more staff members he might encounter before he got anywhere near Robert's office.

Alex hurried up the stairs, two steps at a time. At the top of the staircase two virtually identical hallways led to the left and right. As hard as he tried, Alex couldn't recall where Robert's office was located but then he noticed something that jogged his memory. Halfway along the hallway to his right there was a small table on which stood a bronze bust of one of Robert's illustrious ancestors. Alex was sure that the office was nearby. He crept cautiously along the hallway until he saw the door that he was certain led into Robert's office. The door was partially open, and Alex could clearly see the oak panelling that covered the office's walls. He hurried along the hallway and stopped at the doorway to peer inside. Satisfied that the room was empty, Alex carefully eased the door open and stepped into the office. As soon as Alex was inside the room, the heavy wooden door slammed shut behind him.

"Hello, Alex."

Chapter Twelve
The Terrible Truth

ALEX SPUN AROUND to see Veronica standing by the door. She was wearing another business outfit, this time in dark grey. A huge bald man in a dark suit was standing beside her. Alex panicked but a quick scan of his surroundings told him that there was no way out.

"Get his phone, Lewis," Veronica said to the man in the suit.

He said nothing as he approached Alex.

"Why do you need my phone?"

"Your friend still had her phone when we grabbed her," Veronica replied. "She was trying to send messages but we took it away from her. Lewis turned it off so it couldn't emit a signal. I'll not make the same mistake again. Hand it over."

Alex hesitated but Lewis towered above him. Alex knew that the man would just take the phone by force. He reached into his pocket and handed Lewis the phone. Lewis grinned, accentuating the many lines in his craggy face, before giving the phone to Veronica. She walked over to the desk and sat down in the luxurious black leather chair, placing Alex's phone next to the desktop computer.

"Sit down, Alex."

Veronica gestured at the wooden chair on the opposite side of the desk. Alex walked over and sat down. Lewis stood menacingly in front of the door, barring any possible exit.

"So would you like to tell me what you're doing here?" Veronica asked with a thin smile. "Is this a social call? No, I don't suppose it is. Otherwise you wouldn't have broken the security pad at the main gate. You didn't expect anyone to be here, did you?"

"I saw it on one of the news websites. You were at the airport going to New York."

"Oh, I was at the airport," said Veronica, "but my trip was delayed. The visit to New York was only for a photo op but the deal was all set to be signed and announced the next day anyway. I had tickets for the flight but cancelled them."

Alex's mind was racing. If what Veronica was saying was true, it confirmed that Alexander's future knowledge really was completely unreliable. Alex accepted that it could be caused by how he and Stephanie had been altering the timeline in the present day. However, he also knew that Alexander could be lying or even somehow working with Veronica.

"Do you know why I cancelled my flight, Alex?"

"No idea."

"I was informed by my people that someone was using your dad's credit card."

"How would you know that?"

"I like to stay on top things, Alex, especially if I think that someone could be a threat. We've been keeping a close eye on your dad's movements for quite a while, including phone messages and financial transactions. We've been watching your mom too."

"I think my dad's credit card was stolen," said Alex.

Veronica simply smiled.

"I know that you and your friend were at Castlewood Dynamics when I was visiting my uncle at the hospital, Alex. What were you doing there?"

The desk phone rang before Alex could reply.

"Yes, what is it?" said Veronica, as she answered the phone. "The van's here? Okay, drive around the back and we'll see you there."

She put the phone down.

"Get the girl, Lewis."

He nodded and left the office, closing the door behind him. Veronica briefly picked up Alex's phone. She looked curiously at the unusual icon on the screen before turning off the phone's power.

"I knew that your dad was trying to leave Castlewood and go to work for Hartfield Tech," said Veronica, placing Alex's phone back on the desk. "However, the vital piece of the puzzle that I need for my plans is missing from his laptop."

"What plans?" Alex asked, although he suspected that he already knew the answer.

"It's all very technical," replied Veronica, dismissively, with that same thin smile. "Even for an electronics genius like you. Still, there's one sure way to get the missing data and that's going to be a whole lot easier, now that we've got you."

"What do you mean?"

"You'll see," said Veronica, ominously.

The door opened and Lewis stepped inside, holding Stephanie tightly by the arm.

"Stephanie!" Alex exclaimed. "Are you okay?"

"Yeah, I'm fine," replied Stephanie, wincing slightly at Lewis's grip.

"Let's get going," said Veronica, standing up from her chair.

She scooped up Alex's phone and handed it to Lewis.

"Hang onto this. It's turned off so nobody should be able to track it."

SHE GRABBED ALEX by the arm and they followed Lewis and Stephanie out into the hallway. They all hurried down the staircase and crossed the marble floor into the kitchen. When they reached the loading door at the rear of the mansion, a windowless white van was waiting. Lewis took Stephanie over to the van's back door and opened it. He effortlessly lifted her inside.

"Where are you taking us?" said Stephanie.

"You'll find out soon enough," Lewis replied.

Veronica shoved Alex over to him. Lewis roughly bundled Alex inside the van. A thick blue cloth covered the floor but the inside walls of the van were bare.

"I'll follow in my car," said Veronica. "I'll see you there."

"Sounds good," said Lewis, as he began to close the van doors.

"Wait, where are you taking us?" Alex demanded.

Lewis didn't answer and simply closed the doors.

"We'd better move," said Stephanie, pointing to where a couple of straps were attached to the wall behind the cab. "You don't want to be sliding around in here once we get onto the road."

They shuffled over to the front as Lewis started the engine and the van moved forward.

"Well, at least you're okay," said Alex.

"Yeah," Stephanie replied. "How did you know I was here?"

"Your phone. I had the idea to track your signal and see if I could tell where you were. I'm sure that the police would have thought of that eventually but I saw that you were at least on the way to this area. I figured it was worth a try."

"I slept in and my mom and dad had gone to the gym. I'd just got dressed and had my phone with me when Lewis and another guy came into the house. I was in this van then too and they took my phone so I couldn't call for help. It was still on for a while, I think, before someone decided to turn it off. Or maybe the battery ran out."

Alex smiled. Stephanie forgot to charge her phone on a regular basis.

"Yeah, that wouldn't surprise me."

"They made sure the tablet was turned off too."

"They have the tablet?" said Alex. "But she'll find out that we've been looking into her past and all the companies she works with. There's even evidence of Alexander's messages on there."

"It's fine, Alex. I deleted the history."

"Really? That's not like you."

"Yeah, I know," she smirked. "I figured it might be for the best."

"So what happened when you got to the mansion?"

"They put me in one of the rooms in the basement and tied me up then put some tape over my mouth."

She grimaced at the memory.

"Lewis said that Veronica wanted to talk to me about why we'd been at Castlewood Dynamics. He said that she was on her way back from the airport. They left me alone until you got here. Did they catch you right away?"

"More or less. She was expecting me."

"What do you mean?"

"Well, maybe not expecting me, but they'd found out someone had been using my dad's credit card. That's why she left the airport. She was supposed to be going to sign some important contracts in New York. I didn't think she'd be at the mansion."

"Did you connect with Alexander earlier today?"

"Yes, a couple of times."

"And?"

"I still don't know what to make of all this. He claims that your being kidnapped wasn't supposed to happen. He says that his instructions to us could be altering what he knows as history. I guess it's possible. I mean, I only thought to use the credit card once we'd decided to go the company offices and then I used it again to get to the mansion. That wasn't part of the original timeline and it's what got us caught."

"Yes, but if we were supposed to get captured," said Stephanie, "surely he'd have known that and warned us about it."

"Unless that's all part of his plan."

"What?"

"He could be working with Veronica in the future,

influencing things in this time period."

"That's crazy."

"Maybe," said Alex, with a shrug. "But didn't you say something like that last night? And it's no more crazy than the rest of all this really."

"I guess," Stephanie replied. "And capturing us seems to have given Veronica some ideas that might be part of her big plans. Where do you think they're taking us?"

"No idea," said Alex. "I've given up trying to predict the future."

"So whatever we do, we can't change things?"

"Well, I did wonder if my trying to rescue you proved that I could change the course of events. But now I'm convinced that it's a lost cause. I'm sorry I didn't agree with you earlier."

Stephanie smiled.

THEY CONTINUED THEIR discussion, trying to make sense of what was happening to them, as the van continued its journey. Neither of them had any idea where they were being taken. Eventually the van began slowing down.

"Looks like we might have arrived," said Alex.

The van came to a stop with the engine idling, and they heard what sounded like a heavy overhead door slowly opening.

"Where do you think we are?" asked Stephanie.

"Could be some kind of warehouse maybe?" Alex replied. "I guess we'll find out."

The van began moving again before coming to a halt. The engine was turned off and Lewis opened the van's rear doors.

Chapter Thirteen
The Laboratory

AS HE CLIMBED out of the van, Alex immediately knew where he was. This was the underground parking garage at Castlewood Dynamics. Lewis helped Stephanie out of the van as Veronica's Mercedes drove inside and the main garage door closed behind her. She parked next to the van and got out of the car.

"I hope you had a pleasant journey?" she said icily to Alex and Stephanie, as she closed her car door.

"Where are we?" asked Stephanie.

"Castlewood Dynamics," Alex replied.

"That's right," said Veronica. "I forgot that you've probably been in here before when you came to visit with your dad."

She grabbed Alex's upper arm while Lewis took hold of Stephanie. They all walked over to the elevator doors situated on the nearby wall. Alex assumed that they'd be going up to the main level of the complex although he had no clue regarding what lay in store for him and Stephanie.

However, once the elevator door closed, Veronica took out a plastic card and swiped it on the security panel. The elevator went down instead of up to the main floor of the Castlewood Dynamics building. As far as Alex knew, the parking garage didn't have a lower level.

The elevator quickly descended with no indication of how deep it was heading. It eventually stopped and the doors slid open. Alex found himself in a private section of the Castlewood Dynamics complex that he'd never knew existed. The walls were made of bare steel and reflected the bright overhead lights installed at intervals on the ceiling.

"What is this place?" he asked, as they all stepped out of the elevator.

"I'm not surprised you've never been down here," Veronica explained, as she led him along the gleaming corridor. "Your dad worked in this area sometimes but it was all very confidential, and only a few of our employees know this place even exists. Only a handful of them have the appropriate security clearance. This is where we do all our really secret work. Nothing too sinister, of course, at least not yet."

She smiled.

"My uncle wanted Castlewood Dynamics to have a secure area where we could work on projects and prototypes that would be well hidden from our competitors. You might not be aware of this, Alex, but there's almost as much espionage in the corporate world as there is between countries. It gets pretty crazy at times. This was all my uncle's idea. However, I quickly realized the potential of this area for other purposes as soon as I started working here."

They turned a corner into another identical steel corridor.

"Your dad's contacts with Hartfield Tech were a potential problem regarding the security of our new projects, but I hadn't decided what to do about it yet. My uncle wasn't even vaguely aware of your dad's actions. I would have told him eventually though, if it looked likely that your dad's leaving would cause untold damage to Castlewood."

"And you say that Robert knew about this place?" said Alex.

"Of course, but not what had been happening here recently. He was seriously contemplating retirement as you know and didn't pay much attention to everyday operations anymore. He'd already starting leaving things up to me, which was very convenient. If he ever got curious, it didn't matter since I planned to remove him anyway, sooner or later.

"So you killed him."

"Killed is such a harsh word, isn't it?" said Veronica. "Let's just say I relieved him of his stressful responsibilities, shall we? Ah, here we are."

THEY'D ARRIVED AT a heavy steel door equipped with a security pad on the adjacent wall. Veronica took out a card and swiped it across the pad. The door opened and she and Alex stepped inside, followed by Lewis and Stephanie. The room looked much the same as many of the other Castlewood Dynamics research labs. There were a number of monitors situated around the room's perimeter and several heavy-duty robotic arms attached to the ceiling. Some of the steel tables were covered in various tools and a range of both large and small electronic components. On one table Alex noticed what appeared to be parts of humanoid robots in varying states of repair. At a workstation to his left, it looked as if someone had been working on a drone similar to the ones in Alexander's scenes from the future.

In the shadows in the far corner, a man with thick brown hair sat slumped in a wheelchair. His arms were bound behind him and his face was streaked with dried blood.

"Dad!" Alex exclaimed.

"Oh, my God!" said Stephanie. "What have you done to him?"

They both rushed over to Andrew.

"Relax, he's fine," said Veronica. "Lewis just got a little over enthusiastic with his questioning techniques."

Lewis grinned.

"Dad!" said Alex. "Are you okay? What's happened to you?"

Andrew raised his head at the sound of Alex's voice. Yet Andrew could barely open his eyes before his chin slumped to his chest.

"He's been here since we grabbed him after the car accident," said Veronica. "I have plenty of friends in the police department. They've made sure that your dad's disappearance isn't being pursued too vigorously. We questioned him about the missing data. We tried to determine if he's hidden anything anywhere or even already sent something to Hartfield for safekeeping. When he wouldn't talk, or at least when I didn't believe him, we used what I guess you'd call more persuasive methods."

Andrew's black eyes and the bruises on his face

left Alex in no doubt that his dad had been severely beaten.

"Dad, can you hear me?" Alex asked.

The lab door opened and a tall slim man with short black hair entered. He was carrying a small briefcase and was wearing a dark suit, similar to Lewis. He walked over to where the others were standing in the corner of the lab.

"This is Palmer," said Veronica. "He's something of a genius with drugs that are designed to extract information from people. Once physical beatings didn't work, we tried some truth serums while we had your dad safely hidden away here."

"And Robert knew about this place?" said Alex.

"Well, not about your dad being held here, of course," Veronica replied, smiling. "Like I said, my uncle rarely visited. It was an ideal place to keep your dad, for now at least. I've been able to continue a lot of my earlier work for the company down here."

"But you've only just started working for Castlewood," said Stephanie

"Yes, at this location, since my uncle was looking to take a step back prior to retirement. I've been working for Castlewood for five years in a variety of places, mostly on clandestine projects. Nothing illegal you understand, mostly related to drones and their potential in the civilian arena. However, my uncle didn't want people to know about it in case it ruined the company's image. He was only interested in making money from any research. He was also acutely aware that some employees, including your dad, Alex, as well as some shareholders, weren't entirely in favour of us working on drones after all the negative publicity about their use by the military in different parts of the world. Your dad's work is crucial to the success of so many projects, Alex. We haven't been able to get him to talk, but your arrival at the mansion presented us with an unexpected bonus."

"What do you mean?" said Alex.

Veronica grinned.

"We can torture you instead while he watches. That should get him to tell us what we need to know. Palmer, give him a shot to wake him up."

"That's probably not wise," said Palmer. "We've given him so much already it might be dangerous."

"What's the problem?"

"He's still suffering from all the drugs we gave him earlier. He probably doesn't even recognize his own kid. Torturing the boy or his friend won't do a whole lot of good."

Veronica thought for a moment.

"Very well," she said. "Let's take him to the mine."

"The mine?" said Stephanie.

"Another of my uncle's little secrets," said Veronica. "It's out in the hills, deep in the woods and very discreet. He'd owned the abandoned gold mine for years but never considered doing anything with it until recently. It's only a small facility but it's been an excellent location for me to conduct all my work in private. Most of the projects will probably be done there once my plans get moving. And of course we can use the mind probe there."

"Mind probe?" said Alex.

"Yes," Veronica replied. "An interesting little development that we didn't expect. It was part of our medical research that I'd been supervising and had military applications as well. Drones can be hooked up to people's minds and they can control the machines remotely. We'd only been experimenting with small vehicles with some success but the results were promising. Using the systems for large planes is certainly a possibility. The military in dozens of countries would pay big money for something like that."

"You'd sell out to our enemies?" Alex asked, incredulous.

"It's all about making money, Alex," said Veronica, with a dismissive sweep of her hand. "Even your dad knew that. Despite his noble attitude in public, he knew that Castlewood Dynamics needed to be commercially successful. You can't have any scruples in business these days. If you're standing in the road, eventually you get run over."

"So what's a mind probe?" asked Alex.

"It's something we've been holding back for now," Veronica explained, "but your dad's refused to tell us anything, despite all the drugs we've administered. Your arrival at the mansion opened up the possibility of torturing you in front of him to get him to cave in, but clearly that's not going to work. The mind probe's still experimental but it should get us what we need. Your dad won't survive, of course, but my people in the police department will make sure that his death is never fully investigated and the body's never found. And of course I'll have the crucial data, so that's just fine with me. Your dad simply won't be needed any more."

"You can't do this!" Alex shouted.

"I assure you I can," said Veronica, smiling.

She turned to Lewis and Palmer.

"Okay, let's get moving."

She took Stephanie's arm and began leading her out of the lab. Alex struggled as Lewis grabbed his arm. He was then shocked when Lewis gripped him firmly by the throat. Alex could hardly breathe.

"Don't even think about it," Lewis snarled. "We don't need either of you at all if we're going to use the mind probe. We'll just kill you both once we get to the mine and no one will ever know what happened to you. Understand?"

Alex gulped and nodded as Lewis relaxed his grip. He grabbed Alex's arm and pulled him out into the corridor. Palmer followed, pushing Andrew in the wheelchair.

Once they were in the elevator, Veronica handed Alex's phone to Palmer.

"Have a look at this once we get to the mine," she said. "There's a weird looking app on the screen. This kid's a tech expert so I'd like to make sure he's not been sending signals or anything, even though the phone's turned off."

"Sure, I'll take a look," Palmer replied, slipping the phone into his outer jacket pocket.

THE ELEVATOR ARRIVED at the parking garage. Palmer exited first, pushing the wheelchair. Veronica and Lewis kept hold of Alex and Stephanie as they all walked over to the white van.

"Give me a hand to get him inside," said Palmer.

Lewis took Alex over to where Stephanie was standing with Veronica beside her Mercedes. Veronica's phone rang, and she answered it as Lewis released Alex's arm before walking over to the van. Palmer and Lewis lifted Andrew out of the wheelchair and into the back of the van. Alex could see the top of his phone poking out of Palmer's jacket pocket. Lewis climbed into the van to ease Andrew further inside. Veronica was still talking on her phone as the steel door slowly slid open at the far end of the garage. Alex knew that this was their only chance. He glanced over at Stephanie, who looked terrified. Alex signalled with his eyes toward the garage door. Stephanie swallowed hard but responded with a brief nod to show that she understood. When the garage door was fully open, Alex lunged at Palmer and grabbed the phone.

"Now!" Alex yelled.

Veronica was startled and dropped her own phone onto the concrete floor. Alex and Stephanie raced toward the open garage door. Palmer gave chase, until Veronica called for him to stop.

"Forget it, we don't need them now. I'll have the cops pick them up anyway soon enough. Come on, we need to get him to the mine."

ALEX AND STEPHANIE didn't stop running until they were well away from the underground garage entrance. They hid behind some thick bushes that bordered the lawn of one of the nearby corporate buildings.

"Alex, what—" Stephanie began.

"Quiet!" Alex hissed.

The white van emerged from the parking garage, followed by Veronica's Mercedes. Alex and Stephanie remained still and quiet as the garage door slid closed and the two vehicles drove off in the direction of the main highway.

Chapter Fourteen
Foregone Conclusions

ALEX AND STEPHANIE stepped out from their hiding place. Since it was the weekend, the area surrounding the Castlewood Dynamics headquarters and the other company offices was largely deserted. There was also very little traffic. Alex took out his phone and turned it on.

"So what are we going to do now?" said Stephanie.

"We have to follow them," replied Alex

"But we have no idea where they've gone," Stephanie pointed out. "Even if we did find the place, it could be dangerous. You heard what Veronica said. If your dad dies, she doesn't care about that at all. We could even get killed too."

"But I can't be killed," Alex reminded her. "If Alexander's really my future self and he's sending us messages, I must be alive in the future."

"I don't think we can count on that, Alex," said Stephanie. "No matter what he's been telling us and whether or not he thinks it's correct, the timeline seems to be fluctuating so much now. I don't think we can take anything for granted anymore."

Alex's stomach rumbled.

"Did you eat today?" Stephanie asked.

"No, I was going over to see you and it was getting close to lunchtime by then. How about you?"

"I had only just got up when they grabbed me at the house."

"Let's get something to eat and try to come up with a plan."

THEY WALKED A few blocks from the Castlewood Dynamics building and found a corner coffee shop. They went inside and the place was pretty quiet. A young man was working on his laptop at a table by one of the windows. Three women were just taking their seats at another table beside the counter. A TV on the wall behind the counter was showing one of the local news shows. Alex and Stephanie ordered a couple of cold drinks, along with some cookies and muffins.

The cashier handed Alex his drink and he took a sip. While Stephanie was waiting for her order, a group of people entered the coffee shop. The latest customers were standing at the counter as Stephanie was handed her drink, along with the cookies and muffins. She and Alex immediately noticed the news story on the TV.

In business news, local technology Castlewood Dynamics took another step forward today with the signing of their most lucrative contract yet with the federal government. The contract was signed by Castlewood's representatives in Washington, DC.

Company CEO Veronica Castlewood was unable to attend due to the recent tragic loss of her uncle and company founder Robert Castlewood. The company's success has already spawned many imitators and could perhaps be tempting competitors to take desperate measures. Reports have been coming in of an attempted break-in at the Castlewood Dynamics corporate offices earlier today. Two local children are currently being sought by police.

"Let's get out of here," whispered Alex. "Right now."

Stephanie nodded. They quickly slipped out the door of the coffee shop just in case their names and photographs appeared on the TV screen. They hurried along the sidewalk until they were able to take temporary shelter behind a dumpster in an alley beside a restaurant.

"How could that story be on the news so quickly?" asked Stephanie.

"Veronica has contacts everywhere," Alex replied. "Probably in the police department but certainly in the media. The break-in's a great story, especially since Castlewood's in the news right now because of Robert's death and this government contract."

"So Veronica sent them the information about us?"

"Probably, as soon as they were on the road for the other facility. She told Palmer not to chase us. She's probably hoping that the police will pick us up."

"Here," said Stephanie, handing Alex a muffin and a cookie. "We should eat something."

They sat down on the ground with their backs

against the dumpster.

"So do you really think there's nothing more we can do?" Alex asked, in between bites of his muffin. "To save my dad, I mean."

Stephanie took another bite of her cookie.

"I don't know, Alex. I really don't."

"But if we can somehow find out where this mine is," said Alex, "we can get there in a cab. We might just be able to save him."

"And maybe that's what we're supposed to do."

"Yeah," Alex sighed, "you're right. Everything we're doing might just be part of what Veronica needs to set her plans in motion. Maybe even us staying at home asleep would somehow have been part of how things were supposed to go. I have no idea what we should do. Even doing nothing might be supposed to happen."

"What was it you said?" said Stephanie. "That us using the credit card to get around was what got us caught? That we only learned to do that from Alexander telling us to go to Castlewood Dynamics?"

"Yeah," said Alex "but . . ."

"But then you decided to go to the mansion to try and rescue me. Alexander never put that thought in your head."

"What are you getting at?"

"I mean," said Stephanie, "because you decided that on your own, it seems like nothing we can do can change things. Maybe we were always destined to get taken to Castlewood Dynamics and then escape from the garage, I don't know. But Alexander said your dad had died and now it looks like he's going to die at that mine instead of at the Castlewood Dynamics lab. It's just a different location, that's all. I don't think we're going to be able to change anything."

"We could still try and save him," said Alex, in desperation.

"How?" Stephanie asked. "Yes, we still have the credit card but we have no idea where the mine is."

Alex had to concede that she was right. Despite everything, there was no way they could save Andrew. Alex felt terrible. He'd more or less reluctantly come to terms with the fact that his dad might really be dead then discovered that he was still alive. Losing him like this was like Andrew dying twice. And yet as Stephanie pointed out, there was nothing they could do.

THEY BOTH STOOD up and began walking out of the alley. Before they reached the sidewalk, Alex's phone began to vibrate. He pulled it from his pocket and the special icon was pulsing.

"It's Alexander."

Alex pressed the icon and there was a live video message.

"Thank God you're both okay,"

"What do you want this time?" said Alex.

"Don't hang up," said Alexander. "This is urgent. They've found me."

"Who?"

"Veronica's people. I don't have much time."

There was the sound of raised voices in the background and loud pounding on the door behind him.

"They're here! I've sent you something, but I don't know if it'll get through. Good luck."

Alexander turned away from the screen. Alex and Stephanie heard the sound of the door being broken down followed by two gunshots. Blood was splattered across the screen before it abruptly went blank.

Alex and Stephanie stood in stunned silence near the entrance to the alley.

"Oh my God," said Stephanie. "Is he dead?"

"Looks that way," Alex replied, swallowing hard. "He did say he was in danger of being discovered, remember? He said that he'd moved around a lot and covered his tracks for years. But then he mentioned that being in contact with us made it very risky since he'd had to be in the same place for too long."

"So we're responsible for his death," said Stephanie.

"Don't say that."

"But it's true," she said, her eyes welling with tears. "If he hadn't started this whole thing he'd still be alive."

"Yeah, well, he started it for a reason and knew what he was getting into. If Alexander was ever going to be any help saving my dad, it's all over now."

Chapter Fifteen
A Matter of Trust

AS THEY EMERGED from the alley, a police car drove along the street and stopped outside the coffee shop. Alex and Stephanie darted back into the alley as two officers got out of the car and entered the premises.

"Are they looking for us?" said Stephanie, in alarm.

"I don't know!" Alex snapped.

"Well, it was on the news just now about that break-in at Castlewood."

"I know that but they couldn't possibly have found us that quickly. We only just got here."

"What if the guy who served us tells them something?"

Alex thought for a moment.

"Maybe they're just checking everywhere in this area. We're not that far from Castlewood, after all. Or they even might just be getting coffee."

Stephanie was unimpressed.

"What are we going to do, Alex? It's only a matter of time before we're caught if every cop in the city is looking for us."

"Maybe not every cop," said Alex.

"What are you talking about?"

"We could contact Marino."

"Who?"

Alex reached into his pocket and pulled out his wallet. He then showed Stephanie Officer Marino's business card.

"Marino. She came to the hospital and visited us after the accident. She was at your house talking to your parents after you went missing too."

"I don't know, Alex," said Stephanie, shaking her head. "Veronica said she had connections in the police department. How do you know we can trust Marino?"

"I don't," Alex admitted. "But do you have any other suggestions? Right now we seem to be out of options."

Stephanie sighed then nodded.

"Okay, give her call."

Alex took out his phone and carefully entered Marino's number on the keypad. When prompted, he added the number for Marino's extension.

"It's ringing."

The phone was answered but immediately connected to Marino's voice mail. Alex listened to the recorded message then hung up.

"She's not there?"

"It says that she's in the office, but not at her desk. I don't want to risk leaving a message either with her or with someone at the front desk. We don't know who we're dealing with."

"So what do we do?"

"We have to go over there and see her in person."

Alex quickly studied the address on the card. He used his phone to conduct a quick search for the address of Marino's office. The map showed that it was only a few blocks away.

"Okay, it isn't too far."

THEY CAUTIOUSLY PEERED out of the alley. The sidewalks were somewhat busier with pedestrians than when they'd first arrived at the coffee shop. There was more traffic on the street too, but the police car was gone. Alex and Stephanie both knew that they ran the risk of being recognized at some point on their journey, but each realized that they had little choice.

"So what happens when we get there?" Stephanie asked, as they hurried along the sidewalk. "We just ask to see Marino? What about the person on the front desk? Maybe other cops there might have seen our pictures?"

"I know it's risky," replied Alex. "I'm just hoping that Marino believes us."

"And that she's not working for Veronica."

Alex nodded.

"That too."

They reached an intersection and narrowly missed crossing the street before the traffic lights changed. Alex and Stephanie waited patiently on the sidewalk with several other people. Two police cars approached the intersection, although they didn't appear to be in a hurry. One of the officers in the nearest car began studying the passersby, including those waiting to cross the street.

"Hug me," Stephanie whispered.

"What?" said Alex.

"Hug me."

"What for?"

She didn't wait for his answer. She simply embraced him and pulled Alex's head to the side, facing away from the street.

"What are you doing?" hissed Alex.

"Those cops in the cars are scanning the crowd," she said into his ear. "Keep still so they can't see our faces. They'll think we're making out."

Alex was extremely embarrassed although none of the other people nearby paid any attention.

"Okay, they've gone," said Stephanie, stepping away from him.

Everyone else had already begun crossing the street as soon as the traffic lights changed.

"Right, yes, of course," Alex stammered.

Stephanie winked at him and smiled.

"Let's go."

THEY HARDLY SPOKE for the remainder of the journey as Alex focused on the map directions on his phone. They mingled with the other pedestrians and stayed close to the fronts of shops, restaurants, and other buildings. This made them less visible to passing cars on the street but fortunately they didn't encounter any more police cars or officers on patrol.

"Here we are," said Alex, looking up from his phone. "This is it."

They'd arrived just down the street from the police building housing Marino's office. The wide structure was single story with a parking lot on the right hand side. On the left side of the building, police cars and other vehicles were parked in an area enclosed by a wire fence, although the gate was open to allow officers to drive in and out.

"Let's hope she's in," said Stephanie.

They began walking toward the main entrance, but when they reached the gate of the fenced area, a police officer emerged from the building's front doors. He began walking in their direction, and as he drew closer, Alex and Stephanie recognized Marino's partner, Officer Henderson. He smiled as he stopped to greet them on the sidewalk.

"Alex, isn't it?" he said.

"Hi," said Alex.

"And Stephanie, right?"

"Yeah."

"How are you both doing since the car accident? Are you fully recovered?"

"More or less," said Alex.

"Me too," Stephanie added.

"And how's your mom, Alex? I know it must be very hard for her, not knowing what's happened to your dad. We're doing all we can to find him."

"She's fine," said Alex. "Coping with it as best she can, I guess."

"So what are you two doing here?" Henderson asked, changing the subject.

"We came to see Officer Marino," Alex replied.

"Okay," said Henderson. "Anything I can help you with?"

Alex hesitated, shuffling his feet slightly before Stephanie broke the silence.

"It's kind of a girl's thing," she said, smiling at Henderson. "We really need to speak to a female officer."

"Oh, I see," said Henderson. "Well, I'm not sure if she's in right now but you're very welcome to come in and check."

A call alert sounded from his phone, and he pulled it out of this pocket.

"Excuse me, it's my wife. She rarely calls me at work, so it might be something important about the kids."

He quickly scanned the text and composed a reply before sending the message.

"Okay, let's get you two inside."

Alex and Stephanie began walking toward the building's front entrance.

"No, let's go this way," said Henderson, gesturing toward the fenced lot beside them. "There's a back door that's accessed from the parking lot."

Henderson led them into the lot and closed the gate before they all walked over to the rear entrance to the building. Once inside, he immediately ushered them into a small room. It contained a bare wooden table and four chairs. Against one wall there was a water cooler, along with a metal filing cabinet and a computer on small desk.

"Have a seat," said Henderson.

Alex and Stephanie pulled the chairs out from the table and sat down.

"So you can't tell me what's going on?"

"We'd really rather wait for Officer Marino," said Stephanie.

"No problem, I understand. I'll check and see how long she'll be."

He walked over to the door then turned to face them.

"You two stay in this room. It's probably best if no

one knows you're here until Officer Marino arrives. Don't worry, I'll be right back."

He left the room and closed the door behind him.

"Did he lock it?" Stephanie whispered.

They both stood up and went over to the door. They quickly confirmed that they were locked in.

"Why would he do that?" said Alex, frowning.

"Maybe to stop anyone walking in by accident and finding us here?"

"Okay, but how come he never asked about you being kidnapped?"

"Maybe he's not working on that case?"

"Yeah, but surely he knows about that," said Alex, "even if he wasn't at your house with Marino. After all, he's supposed to be working on my dad's disappearance and you're connected to that."

"You're right, that is strange. How do we know that he's not working for Veronica? She did say she had connections in the police department."

"But he's Marino's partner."

"That doesn't mean anything," Stephanie replied. "We don't really know anything about her either. Didn't Veronica say that her friends would make sure the police investigation into your dad went nowhere? Marino's in charge of the investigation, isn't she, or at least involved in it?"

"You're right," said Alex. "We can't trust these people. We have to get out of here."

They were both startled as Alex's phone received another message. He pulled the phone from his pocket.

"It's Alexander."

"So he's alive?" said Stephanie.

"I don't know. Hang on."

It was a text message rather than a video. Alex pressed the icon but this time there was no message from Alexander. There were only some GPS map coordinates.

"What is it?" Stephanie asked. "Is he okay?"

"No idea. It's some kind of directions."

He showed Stephanie what was displayed on his phone.

"That's the mine."

"How do you know?"

"It must be," said Stephanie. "Look, it's out in the woods, just like Veronica talked about."

They heard footsteps approaching in the hallway outside. Alex shoved his phone back in his pocket just as Henderson opened the door.

"Okay, I've checked with Officer Marino and she's working out of a different office today. I'm going to take you over there. Come on, I've got a car parked out at the back. Don't worry, no one knows you're here."

Alex and Stephanie stood up from the table and followed Henderson out into the hallway. They kept a discreet distance behind him as they made their way to the exit door leading into the parking lot.

"If he's really working for Veronica," Stephanie whispered, "once we get into that police car, we're trapped."

"Well, we can't go anywhere," said Alex. "He locked the gate to the parking lot."

They stepped outside and Henderson was standing beside the open rear door of the police car.

"Here we are," he said.

"Thanks," said Alex.

He climbed into the back of the car. Stephanie slid

in beside him and Henderson closed the door. Alex and Stephanie quickly checked the locks, which were firmly secured on both sides. Henderson settled into the driver's seat and glanced at them in the rearview mirror.

"All settled in back there?" he asked.

"Yeah, we're good," Stephanie replied.

Henderson keyed in some directions to the GPS system, drove up to the gate and put the car into park. He then got out to open the gate.

Alex and Stephanie both leaned forward to get a better view of the computer screen on the dashboard.

"That's the same as the directions Alexander sent us," said Alex.

"Are you sure?"

Alex pulled out his phone. They immediately confirmed that the map coordinates were identical to those displayed on the police car's computer.

"What are we going to do?" Alex asked.

"As soon as we're on the road, and especially before we get out of the city, we'll need a diversion," said Stephanie.

"Like what?"

"You'll see."

Henderson got back into the car.

"Okay," he said. "Officer Marino's working at an office outside town, but hopefully it won't take us too long to get there. There shouldn't be too many other cars around at this time of day."

"Okay," said Stephanie.

"That's fine," Alex added.

The car moved slowly forward through the gate before merging into traffic. Henderson didn't say anything to them as they drove along the city streets, but occasionally checked on his passengers in the mirror. When they passed the coffee shop where they'd been earlier, Stephanie glanced over at Alex and gave him a brief nod.

"Oh, my God," she said. "I'm going to throw up."

"What?" asked Henderson.

"I'm going to throw up. I'm so sorry. It's not usually like this."

"You have to stop the car," said Alex, following her lead.

"What's wrong with her?" Henderson asked, in alarm.

"She gets really travel sick sometimes. It's not usually as bad as this, only when she's on the highway. It brings on her asthma too. Sometimes she can hardly breathe. We have to stop."

"It's not good," said, Stephanie, coughing and covering her mouth with her hand. "I'm going to throw up."

"Okay, okay," said Henderson, impatiently. "Hang on, I'm stopping."

He quickly checked his side mirrors then braked sharply. He parked at the side of the street just beyond the coffee shop, unlocking the doors as he did so. He got out of the car and went to open the back door for Stephanie.

"Here, let me help you," said Henderson, holding out his hand.

"Thanks," Stephanie replied.

She pretended to be having difficulty breathing as she took Henderson's hand and began climbing out of her seat.

"Get the keys if you get a chance," she whispered to Alex.

"What?"

"The car keys, then he can't follow us once we run."

HENDERSON HELPED STEPHANIE to sit down on one of the chairs at the table outside the coffee shop.

"Are you okay now?" he asked.

"I still don't feel good," replied Stephanie.

One of the employees from the coffee shop came outside to see what was happening.

"What's wrong?" the girl asked. "Is she sick? Can I get you some water or something?"

"Yes, please," Henderson replied. "Water would be good."

"Alex, where are my keys?" said Stephanie.

She pretended to cough and almost vomit.

"Your keys?"

"Yes," said Stephanie. "The keys, remember?"

"Oh, yeah. Maybe they're on the back seat?"

Stephanie took a few deep breaths.

"That's it, just breathe," said Henderson. "I'm sure you'll be fine."

Henderson was distracted as some of the coffee shop customers and a handful of passersby asked him what was wrong with Stephanie. Alex went over to the car where the rear door remained open. Henderson's keys were still in the ignition. Alex pretended to be searching on the back seat. He could see that Henderson was still occupied with Stephanie and that people were blocking his view of the car. Alex quickly opened the driver's door and removed the keys from the ignition. He stuffed them into his pocket and rejoined Stephanie at the table. She was taking a sip from a glass of water.

"I couldn't find your keys," he said.

"That's okay," said Stephanie, patting her pocket. "I found them right here."

She laughed a little.

"Are you feeling better now?" asked Henderson.

"Yes, I think so."

"Are you okay to continue? We don't want to be late for our meeting with Officer Marino."

"Just give me a few minutes," Stephanie replied, having another drink.

"Okay, just let me radio in and let her know we might be a little delayed."

Henderson stepped away from the table and walked over to the car. Just before he reached the driver's side door, Stephanie gave Alex another brief nod then leapt to her feet. They both sprinted down the sidewalk, much to the surprise of the people outside the coffee shop.

"Hey!" Henderson yelled.

He raced after them but soon gave up the chase and hurried back to the car. Alex and Stephanie kept running and didn't look back.

Chapter Sixteen
Search and Rescue

ALEX AND STEPHANIE finally stopped running and took refuge at the rear of a convenience store. They hid behind some garbage cans as they heard the sounds of police sirens. They assumed that Henderson would have called for backup once he realized the car keys were missing. Even more police officers were likely to be searching for them now.

"Okay," said Stephanie, catching her breath. "I don't think he followed us, but we can't stay here."

"So where are we going?" Alex asked, breathing heavily.

"We have the directions to the mine."

"We can't know for sure that they're for real."

"True, but why would Alexander have sent us that just before he was killed? It has to be where they're holding your dad."

"It could be another trick too," Alex pointed out.

"If Alexander's dead in the future, he can't have

been working for Veronica, can he? He also can't send us any more false leads or misleading information. And don't forget, Henderson had the same directions too."

Alex thought for a moment.

"I guess we should give it a shot," he said, with a shrug. "Do you think we can risk using the credit card for the cab again?"

"Why not?" replied Stephanie. "Even though Veronica's capable of tracking it, she doesn't think we know how to get to the mine. Chances are that she won't be paying attention since she'll be expecting the police to catch us."

Alex nodded.

"Okay. Let's do this."

He pulled the police car keys from his pocket.

"I guess we don't need these anymore."

He dropped the keys into the nearest garbage can before they headed out to the street to try and hail a cab.

ALEX CAUTIOUSLY STEPPED out onto the sidewalk, quickly scanning his surroundings.

"Maybe you stay hidden and I'll get us a cab," Alex suggested.

"What for?"

"The police are going to be looking for a boy and a girl. You can come out as soon as the cab stops, okay?"

"Good idea," said Stephanie.

Luckily a cab soon appeared and Alex waved frantically to attract the driver's attention. The cab stopped outside the convenience store, and Stephanie hurried out to join Alex on the sidewalk.

"Hi," said Alex. "We need a ride to just outside town."

He showed the driver the map coordinates on his phone as Stephanie anxiously scanned their surroundings.

"Sure," said the driver. "Hop in."

A police car drove around the corner just as Alex and Stephanie climbed into the back seat. They quickly ducked their heads down out of sight of the windows until the police car had passed.

"Are two okay back there?" asked the driver, frowning.

"Yeah, we're fine," Alex replied.

The driver muttered something inaudible before driving away.

ON THE JOURNEY, Alex and Stephanie continued to discuss the impossibilities of their situation. They speculated about the changing timelines and how their actions might all be predetermined. They eventually came to the conclusion that since their current road trip wasn't something that they'd been told to do, they could probably still change the future course of events. The taxi driver occasionally looked at them curiously in his rearview mirror but otherwise seemed oblivious to Alex and Stephanie's conversation.

They only saw a handful of other cars on the road. The journey took over an hour as the daylight steadily faded. Alex continued to study his phone until they eventually reached their destination.

"We're there," said Alex.

He showed Stephanie the map coordinates on his phone.

"Thanks, this is great," he said to the driver.

"What?"

"You can drop us here," said Alex.

"Are you sure?" asked the driver, looking somewhat confused.

"Yes, this is it, thank you."

The driver shrugged and slowed the car to a halt in a pull-in at the side of the deserted road that ran through the woods. Alex gave him the credit card and waited for the driver to process the payment

"Are you kids meeting your parents here or something?" said the driver. "Out here in the middle of nowhere?"

"Yes," said Stephanie, thinking quickly. "Our mom's picking us up here. She's a firefighter and they've been doing some training in the woods over there. We're going to have a tour and spend the night out here."

The driver looked as if he didn't believe a word of what Stephanie was saying.

"Yeah," added Alex, joining in. "We're in the junior firefighter club. I'm sure you've heard of it?"

The driver shook his head and simply shrugged again.

"Okay, if you say so. Have a good day."

Alex and Stephanie got out of the cab as a couple of cars sped by the pull-in, heading in opposite directions. The cab driver gave Alex and Stephanie a curious look before driving away. The cab disappeared around the corner of the twisting road.

"Junior firefighter club?" Stephanie said, with a smirk. "Good one."

"Well, I was just following your lead," Alex replied, grinning.

"So what now?"

"The coordinates on maps these days don't always show places away from main roads and highways, but the directions Alexander sent should take us right to the mine. Let's get out of sight before any more cars drive by here."

They walked into the cover of the woods on the hillside beside the road.

"So," said Stephanie, "have you thought about what we're going to do when we find this place?"

"Not really."

"And if Veronica or anyone else is there? How are we going to get your dad out, presuming he's still alive?"

"I guess we'll find out," said Alex. "I just hope the phone battery stays charged for long enough. The power level's pretty low."

"What about cell phone coverage once we get further from the road?"

"That's going to be patchy, at best. There must be some cell towers along the road so that drivers can use their phones out here, but I don't know how effective they'll be in the woods."

THEY FOLLOWED THE map directions on Alex's phone for around twenty minutes. When they emerged from the woods, they'd reached a dry dirt road. There were vehicle tracks but it was hard to tell how recent they were.

"There's nothing here," said Stephanie.

"There has to be," Alex countered. "The coordinates lead right to this place."

"Maybe Alexander was leading us astray, even with his final message?" said Stephanie.

Alex almost threw his phone to the ground in frustration, but then they heard a vehicle engine. He and Stephanie dropped back into the cover of the trees as the white van from Castlewood Dynamics emerged out of nowhere from some thick bushes and sped along the dirt road. Lewis was driving the van and there appeared to be someone else with him in the front passenger seat. However, the van drove by too quickly for either Alex or Stephanie to get a good look at the other occupant.

"There must be a concealed entrance nearby," said Alex. "Come on."

"Alex, wait," said Stephanie. "Look."

She pointed upward. Two drones were hovering high among the treetops. The small robot aircraft resembled the ones that they'd seen patrolling the future city streets in the scenes that Alexander had shown them on the TV.

"What are they doing?" Stephanie whispered.

"Patrolling the area, by the looks of things," replied Alex. "Perhaps they do that every time the van or anything else goes in and out of the mine."

"They look a lot like those futuristic ones."

"They're probably prototypes that Veronica's developing here and testing out in the woods."

The drones were scanning the area around the road. Eventually, after hovering perilously close to where Alex and Stephanie were hiding, the drones swiftly flew away and out of sight.

ALEX AND STEPHANIE hurried over to where the van had emerged. Behind the bushes there was a pair of steel doors in the rock face, along with a small security pad.

"How do we get inside?" said Stephanie.

"No problem," Alex replied. "This looks like the system that controlled the main gate back at the mansion. It should be easy enough for us to access."

He eased the cover from the security pad but the circuitry was more complex than the device he'd hacked previously.

"Want me to take a look?" said Stephanie.

"Okay, but don't be long. We don't know how long those drones will be patrolling for."

Stephanie went to work on the security panel. Alex nervously scanned the sky above the treetops, watching for the drones.

"Any progress?"

"Close," Stephanie replied. "Just a few more minutes."

Then Alex saw them. The drones had returned.

"I don't think we have a few more minutes," said Alex. "Look."

Stephanie glanced over her shoulder and saw the drones heading toward the mine entrance.

"They're coming right for us!" she exclaimed. "They're going to see us!"

"Get down!" said Alex.

He dropped to the ground under the bushes, pulling Stephanie down with him. They kept perfectly still as the drones approached the rock face. At that very moment the drones skimmed down to the height of the bushes and the steel doors slid open. The drones flew through the doorway and travelled down the long passage that led into the heart of the mine.

"Quick!" said Alex. "Before it closes."

He and Stephanie scrambled to their feet and

slipped inside the mine just before the heavy doors clanged shut behind them.

Chapter Seventeen
Into the Depths

THE PASSAGE INTO the interior of the old mine was paved with stone slabs but the walls were composed of bare rock. There were no lights on the ceiling although lighting panels were installed at intervals along the wall. Alex and Stephanie steadily crept forward, hoping that the drones wouldn't fly back in their direction. If they did, Alex and Stephanie had nowhere to hide and would immediately be discovered. Eventually the passage's bare walls gave way to steel panels that closely resembled those on the walls in the depths of the Castlewood Dynamics headquarters where Andrew had been held prisoner.

They didn't see any doorways and there was no sign of anyone in the converted mine. The facility also appeared to be quite small. Eventually, Alex and Stephanie arrived at another heavy steel door. This one didn't have a security pad on the adjacent wall.

"What do you think?" said Alex.

"Let's give it a try," Stephanie replied.

They eased the door open with some difficulty and entered a large room filled with a variety of scientific equipment. It was similar to the secret laboratory that they'd been inside at the company headquarters. At the far end of the room, Andrew was lying on an operating table.

"Dad!" Alex exclaimed.

He and Stephanie rushed over to where Andrew lay. His face had been cleaned of blood but was still heavily bruised. Andrew was unconscious and was connected to a number of surrounding machines by a myriad of wires, cables, and tubes. Some of the equipment appeared to be monitoring his vital signs. Ominously, there was a semi-circular helmet made of grey metal covering the top of his head. The helmet was connected to a computer with a very large screen although the monitor wasn't activated. Alex immediately reached over to begin detaching some of the tubes and wires.

"Alex, no," said Stephanie, grabbing his arm. "You could kill him. We don't know what any of these connections do."

"But do you think he's okay?"

"He's still breathing, but it looks like they've been working on him already."

"And do you think they got all the information they wanted?"

"I don't know, Alex," said Stephanie. "This machinery is as much of a mystery to me as it is to you. Veronica's people haven't been gone long though."

She picked up a paper coffee cup from the nearby counter.

"The coffee's still warm."

"So, they could be coming back here at any time?"

"Yes," said Stephanie. "And if they'd already got the information they needed, your dad would be dead by now. Remember what she said about that."

"You're right. We have to get him out of here."

"Okay, but you have to give me some time to try and figure everything out, Alex. Disconnecting him from this stuff could easily kill him if we get it wrong."

"Fine," said Alex. "But be as quick as you can. As far as we know, there's only one way out of here back into the woods if anyone returns."

STEPHANIE SAT IN one of the chairs and began working on the different machines that surrounded the area where Andrew lay unconscious. Alex studied the other equipment in the lab. The mind probe looked relatively inconspicuous but he was sure that it was a deadly weapon that Veronica wouldn't hesitate to use on her enemies in the future. Alex had no idea what important scientific information his dad might possess. Yet Alexander had mentioned that Veronica learned something at this point in history, presumably from Andrew, which led to her dominating the entire world in the coming decades. Alex shuddered when he recalled the gunshots and the blood on the screen when they'd received Alexander's final message. Alex felt decidedly unnerved at the thought of his own future death. But then this entire adventure had been utterly bizarre, to say the least.

While Stephanie was engaged in very elaborate procedures on the various keyboards and consoles,

Alex examined the lab's monitors. Some of them showed different views of the facility, including the entrance from the woods and the underground passage that Alex and Stephanie had travelled along. There also seemed to be another entrance for vehicles, presumably located somewhere on the opposite side of the mine. Two of the cameras were positioned at a parking area situated somewhere in the facility. Alex was relieved to see that it was empty and that Veronica's Mercedes was absent. Some cameras were focused on the approach to the mine entrance along the dirt track. There were even views of the area where Alex and Stephanie had earlier arrived in the cab. Alex watched a single car drive by but the road was otherwise deserted.

Stephanie finished typing on the keyboard and stood up from the chair.

"I think I've got it," she said, turning to Alex.

"Are you certain?"

"No, Alex, I'm not, but I'm as sure as I can be. Help me to disconnect these things."

They carefully uncoupled Andrew from everything that connected him to the machinery. Andrew began to regain consciousness, at one point opening his eyes. However, he didn't seem to recognize either of them and remained very groggy as a result of all the drugs he'd been given.

As they removed the last few wires, Alex noticed something on one of the counters.

"That's my dad's laptop."

The computer was connected to some of the equipment that had been linked to the mind probe helmet.

"I'd better check it out," said Stephanie.

"Why?" Alex asked. "If there were anything on there they wouldn't have needed to torture my dad and bring him here."

"Maybe, but Veronica might have been using this laptop and left something on there."

"But what good will that do us?"

"I don't know!" Stephanie snapped. "Just let me try. Look after your dad. If he's at least slightly awake, it'll be easier for us to get him out of here and into the woods."

Stephanie conducted a quick check of the laptop. Alex helped Andrew to sit up on the operating table.

"Dad? Dad, can you hear me? It's Alex."

There seemed to be a glimmer of recognition as Andrew narrowed his eyes and studied Alex's face.

"Alex?" he mumbled. "I don't know . . . I mean . . ."

He appeared confused as he peered around the lab, attempting to make sense of his surroundings.

"What . . . what's happening?"

"Don't worry, Dad. We're going to get you out of here."

Alex turned to Stephanie.

"Anything yet?"

"Everything on here's password protected," replied Stephanie. "Let me have another try."

Alex glanced over at one of the monitors. Veronica's Mercedes had arrived at the parking area, followed by the white van.

"We've got company."

"What?"

"Veronica's here, with the others. We have to go."

"Wait. I might still find something."

On the monitor, Alex watched as Veronica emerged from her car and chatted briefly with Lewis and Palmer as they got out of the van

"There's no time," said Alex, struggling to ease Andrew up from the operating table.

Veronica and the others could no longer be seen on the monitor that was focused on the parking area.

"Stephanie!" Alex exclaimed. "They're on their way!"

"Wait!" she said. "I've found something."

She opened a file and quickly scanned the contents.

"There are some financial records and stock market details on here."

"So what?" said Alex, in frustration. "Help me with my dad."

He'd managed to get his dad to stand, but Andrew was still very unsteady on his feet. Alex leaned him up against one of the nearby consoles and held onto Andrew's arms to stop him from falling.

"Alex, these documents might be very incriminating," said Stephanie. "These are all the accounting records of Veronica's dealings with the other companies we learned about. I guess she never considered these records to be important enough to keep them hidden."

"But what use are they to us right now?"

"I've no idea if this material's anything illegal, but it's certainly a smoking gun. She'd have a hard time explaining some of this stuff, for sure."

"Okay, fine. Let's take the laptop with us."

"It's hooked up to everything. It might set off some alarms or even wipe all the data."

On one of the monitors, Alex saw Veronica and the others walking along a corridor. Stephanie saw them too.

"Oh, my God," she gasped.

"So what do we do?" said Alex.

"We have to leave the laptop. Let's get your dad out of here. They could be here at the lab at any minute."

"Wait," said Alex. "I still have Marino's card."

"What do you mean?"

Alex pulled his wallet from his pocket and handed Marino's card to Stephanie.

"It's got her email address on it. Can you send her those documents by email?"

Stephanie grinned.

"Brilliant idea, Alex."

She accessed the email on the laptop. On the monitor, Alex saw that Veronica and the others were now walking along a different corridor, which had bare rock walls. He had no idea how close they were to the lab.

"Hurry up. They're probably almost here."

Stephanie typed in Marino's address.

"Do I add a message and say it's from us?"

"Just send it," said Alex. "We'll work all that out later, if we get out of here in one piece."

She quickly attached the document containing the financial records to the email and hit send.

"Did it go?" asked Alex.

"Yes, let's get going. Can your dad walk okay?"

"I think so, but we'll both need to help him."

They each placed one of Andrew's arms across their shoulders and headed for the exit. Andrew stumbled a couple of times but did his best to help. Struggling to support Andrew between them, Alex and Stephanie reached the laboratory door. They then moved as fast as they could along the passageway that led to the exit back into the woods.

"Do you think there's an access code from this side?" asked Stephanie, as they approached the firmly closed steel doors.

"Let's hope not, we don't have time to hack anything."

When they reached the doors, they were relieved to find a simple activation button on the wall. Stephanie pressed it and the doors opened.

"Come on, before it closes again," she said.

They both adjusted their hold on Andrew before they all stumbled out into the early evening sunlight.

Chapter Eighteen
No Escape

ALEX AND STEPHANIE followed the dirt track since it was easier than trying to move through the tangled woods while supporting Andrew. They all had to rest once they'd travelled a safe distance from the mine entrance. They moved just off the road and into the cover of the nearby bushes. Alex sat his dad down beside a tree, and Andrew began to fully regain consciousness.

"Alex?" he mumbled. "Is that really you? And Stephanie?"

"Yes, Dad it's us. Are you okay?"

Andrew frowned as he rubbed his forehead.

"I have a terrific headache. What did they do to me?"

"Something called a mind probe," said Alex. "They were using it to get information out of you after all those drugs and the beatings failed."

Andrew winced at the memory.

"So what happened after the car crash?" Stephanie asked.

"When I woke up, I was at the lab deep under the Castlewood headquarters. I'd worked down there a few times but it was a very restricted area. Veronica was planning all sorts of things with my latest breakthroughs and she'd learned that I planned to leave for Hartfield. They'd got most of my research but there was some data that I'd decided to hang onto."

"What for?" Alex asked.

Andrew paused for a second and rubbed his forehead again.

"I didn't like the direction in which Veronica seemed to be heading. I was really worried that she'd been using my work for something sinister. They had my laptop so they secured some of my secret data, but when I wouldn't tell them anything they tried to persuade me. That Palmer guy injected me with all sorts of things."

"Well, at least you're safe now," said Stephanie, smiling.

Andrew looked all around him with a puzzled expression on his face.

"And where are we anyway?" he asked.

"In the woods outside of town," replied Alex. "Castlewood has a secret facility in an abandoned gold mine."

"Really? I never knew anything about that."

"No, they kept it secret from just about everyone," Alex explained. "Robert set it up a while ago but Veronica's been able to use the place for her own plans."

"Is Robert involved? I can't believe he'd do

something like this?"

Stephanie looked over at Alex before she replied.

"I'm afraid Robert's dead. He officially collapsed on a golf course and died in hospital, but we know that Veronica poisoned him."

"What?" said Andrew, in astonishment. "I don't understand. What do you mean Robert's dead?"

"I'm sorry, Dad," Alex replied. "I know he . . ."

They were interrupted by the sound of a faint humming in the distance.

"Wait," said Stephanie. "Get down. Those drones are back."

"Drones?" said Andrew.

"Get down, Dad."

They all took cover beneath under the nearby shrubs and undergrowth as the two small robot aircraft skimmed the treetops as they approached. Alex, Stephanie, and Andrew all held their breath as the drones hovered directly above where they were concealed. Stephanie almost gasped as the drones suddenly descended and hovered only a few feet above the road. They were much closer than they'd been last time when Alex and Stephanie had first spotted them in the woods. The drones weren't equipped with the pale blue beam that the futuristic models had deployed, but appeared to be scanning the area with multiple miniature cameras. They were also armed with some kind of gun, which was attached underneath the drone's bodywork and had the ability to swivel in all directions. The drones abruptly stopped their scanning and ascended to the treetops then flew away, heading in the direction of the main road.

Alex and Stephanie quickly got to their feet then

helped Andrew to stand.

"Those looked like some of the prototype drones we've been working on," said Andrew, as he leaned against the tree. "I had no idea any of them were operational. Those looked like they were armed too. We never planned for anything like that."

"Veronica has big plans for those in the future," said Stephanie.

"What do you mean?" Andrew asked.

Alex glanced over at Stephanie and shook his head. He was determined that his dad wouldn't learn anything about their encounters with Alexander from the future.

"How did you find out what was happening anyway?" asked Andrew. "And how did you manage to find this place in the woods?"

"We'd better get moving," said Alex, quickly changing the subject. "If those drones are flying, Veronica must be looking for us. We need to get to the road and flag down a passing car."

"Do you know the way?" asked Andrew.

"Yeah, the coordinates we used to get here are still in my phone. We'll just backtrack."

"Can you walk?" Stephanie asked.

"Yes, I think so," replied Andrew.

"You can lean on me if you need to, Dad," said Alex, with a smile.

THEY ALL STEPPED out of the bushes and onto the dirt road.

"Shouldn't we be staying more out of sight in the woods?" asked Stephanie.

"Maybe," Alex replied, "but we'll probably reach the main road quicker if we go this way. The van drove down here so we know that the road can't be too far. It'll be easier for you too, Dad. Hopefully we won't run into those drones again."

They all began moving down the road, with Alex and Stephanie holding Andrew's arms. He was now able to walk a little easier but still needed their support. Yet, they hadn't travelled that far before they all heard an ominous humming in the air above them. One of the drones was back. It quickly dropped to their level and hovered in the air a few feet ahead of them, blocking their path. Coloured lights on the drone's bodywork flickered, and the gun underneath it turned until it was pointed directly at them.

"What do we do?" said Stephanie.

"Split up," Alex replied. "It can't shoot all of us at once."

Alex pulled Andrew into the shrubs at the edge of the road while Stephanie darted to the opposite side. Andrew stumbled and fell into the undergrowth. The drone headed directly for Alex, its weapon prepared to fire.

"Alex!" Stephanie yelled.

She picked up a large rock from the side of the road and threw it at the drone. The rock smashed one of the drone's rear cameras before ricocheting against a tree. The drone immediately spun around and turned its weapon to face Stephanie. She dove into the bushes as the drone fired an energy beam, which blasted a gaping hole in the tree beside her. Stephanie scrambled to her feet as the drone flew toward her and fired again, narrowly missing her head as Stephanie fell to the ground. The drone swiftly advanced and was only a few feet away from where she lay, preparing to fire, when Alex appeared behind it and hit the drone hard with the rock. The drone fell to the ground, and Alex smashed it several more times until the drone's lights were all extinguished.

"You okay?" he asked, catching his breath.

"Yeah," said Stephanie, with a sigh of relief. "Thanks, that was close."

Alex reached out his hand and helped her up. They were both startled when an energy beam hit the tree beside them, causing two branches to fall.

"It's the other one!" Alex yelled. "Split up!

They ran in opposite directions, confusing the drone. For a second, it didn't seem able to decide which way to go, but then turned to pursue Alex. Alex weaved and dodged as he ran through the forest. The drone kept firing at him as it zipped between the trees, steadily gaining on him. However, when Alex abruptly changed direction, the drone couldn't adjust its trajectory in time, crashing into a tree at high speed and dropping to the ground. Alex cautiously crept over to where the drone lay. The machine was silent and most of its lights were no longer lit. The drone's gun also appeared to have been severely damaged in the collision with the tree.

"Is it broken?" asked Stephanie when she joined him.

"Let's hope so."

"Where's your dad?"

"Just over there."

They hurried back to the road to where Andrew was emerging from the undergrowth.

"Are you two hurt?"

"We're fine, Dad. Let's get moving."

"How did you beat them? Those drones looked

deadly. And what were those guns firing? Lasers or something?"

"Well, they're supposed to be pretty sophisticated machines," Alex replied. "I guess they just aren't designed to fly around where there are lots of trees."

"Maybe what just happened means someone will make improvements in the future?" said Stephanie.

She winked at Alex.

"Are there any more of those things around here?" asked Andrew.

"We've only seen two so far here in the woods," Alex replied. "I guess these might not have been the same ones that we saw earlier though."

"Either way, let's just focus on getting to the main road, in case there are any more drones on patrol," said Stephanie.

THEY WERE ABOUT to resume their journey when Veronica's Mercedes roared into view on the dirt track. The car screeched to a halt directly in front of them. Veronica immediately got out, brandishing a handgun.

"Did you really think you'd get away?" she snarled, waving the gun as she walked toward them.

"Veronica," said Andrew, still struggling to stand. "Put the gun away."

"Shut up, Andrew. I don't want to shoot you, but I will if I need to. You can be sure of that."

Veronica turned to face Alex and Stephanie.

"Did you really think that I wouldn't come after you? We have cameras all over the woods, as well as on the road. We have those camera-equipped armed drones in the air as well. How did you expect to get away?"

"The police will arrest you," said Stephanie.

Veronica simply smiled.

"Oh, I know what you sent to that police officer. Unfortunately Marino's not on my payroll, but it won't make any difference anyway. Those are just financial records, nothing more. And as I'm sure you know by now, Henderson's working for me. There's no guarantee that Marino will ever see that email you sent her."

"But those records still show everyone what you've been up to."

"Up to? Don't be a fool, girl. They just indicate some of the many companies that I've been dealing with over the last few years. I've done nothing wrong."

"They'll be able to see your plans for the future," said Alex, not wanting to let on what he and Stephanie knew.

"Even if they do, it won't matter. There's nothing in those records to incriminate me. They won't even arrest me for killing you three."

"What do you mean?" said Alex.

"The police suspect that your dad's already dead anyway," Veronica explained. "When we kill him now no one will ever know what happened. We'll do something different with you two. Lewis and Palmer are on their way. I just wanted to arrive here first to make sure that you didn't get away. It's so easy to dispose of bodies, when you have all the right connections."

"You can't do this!"

"Oh, but I can, Alex," said Veronica. "You're so naive, just like your dad. Once you're all dead, I'll be leaving the country on a private plane. My lawyers and other friends will deal with everything while I stay out of harm's way. I'll even be able to run things at Castlewood Dynamics from an offshore location. I'm sure you know that my family has many friends in high places, including in the justice system."

Veronica took out her phone to call Lewis and Palmer. She was still pointing the gun but was momentarily distracted as she keyed in the phone number. Alex seized his chance and lunged at her.

"Alex, no!" yelled Andrew.

Alex grabbed Veronica's arm, and Stephanie immediately joined his assault. Veronica dropped her phone before the call was completed. She and the children violently struggled with each other as they all staggered closer to the edge of the woods at the side of the road.

"Alex!" Andrew exclaimed.

He attempted to intervene but his legs were still too weak, and he tripped and fell to the ground.

"Let go!" screeched Veronica. "I'll kill you all!"

As she attempted to fight off Alex and Stephanie, there was a single gunshot. Alex and Stephanie let go of Veronica, who stumbled backward. She fell into the undergrowth and hit her head on a small boulder, dropping the gun. There was a trickle of blood running down Veronica's left temple, and she wasn't moving.

"Alex!" said Andrew, finally managing to struggle to his feet. "Stephanie! Are you okay?"

"Yeah," said Alex, still breathing heavily.

"Thank God you're both okay," said Andrew, as they all embraced. "What about her?"

Stephanie reached down and gently placed her fingers on Veronica's neck.

"She's alive, although I don't know how badly hurt she is."

"We have to get out here," said Alex. "She said those guys were on their way to meet her."

"What about the gun?" asked Stephanie, pointing to where the weapon had fallen at the edge of the bushes. "In case she wakes up sooner rather than later?"

Alex thought for a moment then grabbed a short branch from the side of the road.

"What's that for?" asked Stephanie.

"I don't want to leave any fingerprints, just in case."

He slid the branch through the trigger of the gun to pick it up. He then flung the gun as far as he could into the forest.

"There," he said. "Even if she does wake up while we're still here in the woods, she won't be as dangerous."

THEY MOVED BACK into the trees to stay hidden in case Lewis and Palmer arrived in the van. Alex and Stephanie helped Andrew to walk as they travelled as quickly as possible through the woods until they reached the main road. A couple of cars sped by just before they emerged from the woods.

"We only just missed them," said Stephanie, as they all stepped out onto the gravel at the side of the road.

"There'll be others soon, don't worry," said Alex.

"I hope you're right," Stephanie replied. "This road's usually pretty quiet most of the time. I just hope another car comes by before Lewis and Palmer have a chance to find us."

They crossed over to the pull-in area where Alex and Stephanie had been dropped off by the cab earlier that day. Andrew sat down to rest on one of the larger boulders.

"Okay, now what?" he asked.

"We wait for a car," replied Alex.

"Listen," said Stephanie. "It sounds like one's coming,"

She moved to the edge of the road, waving her arms frantically as an older model blue car came around the corner. The car slowed down, turned into the pull-in, and stopped. A middle-aged man wearing a t-shirt, shorts, and a baseball cap stepped out from the driver's seat.

"What happened to you guys?" said the man, as he approached them.

"We were out hiking and our dad twisted his ankle," said Alex.

He noticed that the man was carefully studying Andrew's face, noting all his fresh bruises.

"Are you going to be okay?" the man asked Andrew.

"Yes, I think so," he replied. "I'll be fine. I just need to go home and get fixed up."

The man peered further along the road in both directions.

"Where's your car parked?" he asked.

Alex hesitated, unsure of what to say.

"My mom dropped us all off here this morning," said Stephanie, thinking quickly.

"Does she know what's happened to your dad?" the man asked.

"No," replied Stephanie. "My dad wouldn't let us bring our cell phones and his battery died. We only just managed to get him all the way to the road, hoping someone like you would stop and help us."

The man continued to study Andrew's face. To Alex's alarm, the man also glanced curiously over at the spot where they'd emerged from the woods. Stephanie noticed too and gave Alex a wink.

"Oh, Dad!" she exclaimed, hugging Andrew. "It's all my fault you got hurt! I'm so sorry."

She instantly burst into tears, which grabbed the man's attention.

"Okay, okay," he said, appearing somewhat unnerved at Stephanie's emotional outburst. "Let's get you guys home."

Stephanie gave Alex another wink as the man helped Andrew to stand. The man supported Andrew as he walked over to the car. Alex and Stephanie helped to ease Andrew into the passenger seat. They then climbed into the back of the car.

"I'm Frank, by the way," said the man, offering Andrew his hand.

"Andrew Mitchell," said Andrew, shaking Frank's hand. "This is Alex and Stephanie."

"Pleased to meet you both," said Frank, turning to face the back seat before turning the key in the ignition. "So where am I taking you?"

"We should probably take my dad to a hospital to get checked out," said Alex.

"Yeah," Stephanie agreed. "Just to make sure nothing's broken."

"Okay," said Frank. "Not a problem."

He drove out of the pull-in and onto the road. They hadn't travelled far when just ahead of them, the white van roared out of the woods through the exit from the dirt track. The tires screeched loudly as the van sped past them on the opposite side of the road.

"Wow, looks like someone's in a hurry," said Frank.

Alex and Stephanie nervously looked out of the car's back window. They breathed a sigh of relief as the white van continued speeding away in the opposite direction before it vanished out of sight around the corner.

Chapter Nineteen
The Road to Recovery

IT WAS GETTING dark as they approached the hospital. Alex had tried calling his mom a couple of times from the car to let her know what had happened. However, she hadn't answered and he didn't leave a message. He decided he'd wait until they'd safely arrived at the hospital before he'd try Angela again.

Frank parked the car in the short-term loading zone outside the entrance to the hospital's Emergency department. He then helped Andrew out of the passenger seat.

"Are you guys going to be okay?" asked Frank. "Did you want me to come in with you?"

"No, I think we'll be fine, thanks," Alex replied. "We can take it from here."

"Thanks again for all your help," said Andrew, shaking Frank's hand.

"No problem," Frank replied. "Best of luck."

He got back into the car and waved to them all as

he drove away.

STEPHANIE WENT OVER to grab one of the hospital wheelchairs that were standing beside the Emergency entrance.

"There's no need for that," said Andrew, dismissively, as she eased the wheelchair toward him.

"Come on, Dad," said Alex. "You're still unsteady on your feet."

"Fine," said Andrew.

He scowled then smiled at both of them as he sat down in the wheelchair.

"You'd better try your mom again, Alex."

"Yeah, I know."

Alex took out his phone and this time Angela picked up straight away.

"Mom, it's Alex."

"Alex? Where are you? I'm sorry, I only just saw that you'd called a couple of times earlier. My phone's been really weird today."

"We found Dad."

"What? What do you mean? I don't understand. You found your dad? Is he okay?"

"He's fine," Alex replied, smiling over at Andrew. "We're at the hospital."

"Which one?"

"The same one as before."

"But is he okay?"

"He's fine, Mom, honestly. They're just going to check him out. We can talk about this once you get here."

"I'm on my way," said Angela, hanging up.

"What did she say?" Andrew asked.

"She's heading over here. Let's get you inside."

Stephanie grabbed the wheelchair handles and began pushing Andrew toward the revolving door at the hospital's entrance.

"Can you take him to the reception desk?" said Alex. "I just need to check something."

"What?" Stephanie asked.

Alex edged back a couple of steps and tilted his head, indicating that Stephanie should join him.

"What is it?"

"I need to call Marino," Alex whispered. "I just don't want Dad to hear me."

Stephanie nodded and went back to Andrew. As they entered the Emergency department, Alex made another phone call.

"Officer Marino? It's Alex Mitchell."

"Alex? Where are you? What's going on? I got a message from your dad, or at least from his email."

"We found him. He's here at the hospital, the one where we first met."

"What? Where did you find him?"

"It's a long story, believe me," said Alex. "It'll be easier to explain in person."

"I'll be right there."

ALEX MADE HIS way into the hospital. Stephanie and Andrew were sitting in the waiting area directly across from the reception desk.

"We've checked in," said Stephanie, as Alex approached. "They said someone's coming to see us in a minute."

A nurse emerged through a pair of doors beside the desk.

"Mr. Mitchell?" she said.

"Yes," replied Andrew.

"What happened to you?" she asked, studying the wounds and bruises on Andrew's face.

"It's a complicated story," Andrew replied.

"Well, we'll get you fixed up," said the nurse.

She took hold of the handles and gently turned the wheelchair around. She then wheeled Andrew through the double doors. Alex and Stephanie followed the nurse as she steered Andrew's wheelchair along the corridors. The hospital was relatively busy with a variety of medical staff, technicians, patients, and their family members. Alex and Stephanie stayed a few paces behind the nurse.

"What did you and Dad tell them?" asked Alex.

"We said he'd been attacked and robbed," Stephanie replied. "The woman at the reception desk asked for more details but I said that the police were coming here. I hope you spoke to Marino."

"I did. She's on her way."

"Okay, Mr. Mitchell," said the nurse ahead of them. "It's just through here."

They entered a large room containing a number of beds, some of which were curtained off. The nurse wheeled Andrew toward one of the patient areas and pulled the curtain aside.

"Do you need help?" she asked Andrew, as she parked the wheelchair beside the bed.

"No, I'll be fine," said Andrew.

He carefully stood up from the wheelchair and lay down on the bed.

"Okay," said the nurse. "One of the other nurses will be here shortly to check on you and get the drip connected."

"Thanks," said Andrew.

The nurse left, and Andrew immediately turned to Alex and Stephanie.

"So how did you find me anyway? Didn't you say that mine in the woods was a secret facility?"

"How much do you remember, Dad?" asked Alex. "After the car crash in the rainstorm?"

"I don't remember how I got there but they kept me in that laboratory under the company headquarters at first and asked me all sorts of questions. One of Veronica's accomplices was pretty rough, trying to beat me into submission. But I think I was more afraid of the other one, Palmer, the guy who injected me with all sorts of drugs. After he started doing that, I don't remember much at all until I was at the mine. How did you find that place?"

Alex paused before answering.

"Mom and I never accepted that you might be dead," he began. "We were both convinced that you'd be found eventually, but Stephanie and I did some research too."

"What kind of research?" asked Andrew.

Alex looked over at Stephanie for some inspiration.

"We were both suspicious of Veronica," she added, "especially after Robert died. It was just too sudden. He was in very good shape."

"Yes, we were going to do that half-marathon for charity," said Andrew, sighing. "I still can't believe he's gone."

"We had no proof," Alex said. "But it just seemed to us to be very convenient that he was dead and that she was taking over the company so quickly. We looked into her business dealings."

161

"We also went to Castlewood Dynamics," said Stephanie.

"What for?"

"Robert and Veronica came to the house to see how Mom and I were doing," Alex explained. "Veronica took your laptop away with her. She said she needed to check a few things on there."

"But she has no authority to do something like that," said Andrew.

"That's what we thought," Stephanie added. "Even if they assumed you might be dead at that point, at least officially. We managed to get into the offices at Castlewood but we couldn't find the laptop. We learned about Robert's death just as we were leaving the building."

"We decided to go to the police and talk to them," Alex continued. "A couple of officers visited us here at the hospital after the accident so we decided to go and see them. We wanted to talk to Officer Marino, who came to see us, but she wasn't around so we saw her partner, Officer Henderson."

"And he helped you?"

Stephanie shook her head.

"At first it seemed that way, but he was going to take us to a place outside town. We saw the coordinates on the GPS in the police car. We knew that he was working for Veronica. We escaped and got a cab out to the woods and then went to the mine. The rest you know."

"Working for her?" said Andrew, looking confused. "I don't understand."

"Veronica had friends in the police department who were helping her, Dad," said Alex.

"I can't believe this. The police?"

"Yes," Stephanie added. "She had them make sure that your disappearance wasn't being investigated properly. I think she thought that eventually you'd be declared dead and it'd all be forgotten."

"Okay, Mr. Mitchell," said a male nurse, as he arrived at the bedside. "I just need to get you hooked up to the drip and do a few tests. Do you kids want to go and wait in the reception area? This won't take too long."

"Dad?" said Alex.

"It's okay," Andrew replied. "You two wait out there. Maybe your mom will be here soon and you can send her in here to see me?"

Chapter Twenty
Telling Stories

ANGELA ARRIVED JUST as Alex and Stephanie sat down in the reception area. She hurried over and gave them both a big hug.

"Where's your dad? Are you going to tell me what's going on?"

"It's a long story, Mom," said Alex. "Why don't you go and see Dad first?"

He didn't want Angela to be there when Marino arrived at the hospital.

"Yes, you're probably right," she said. "Do I need to check in with anyone?"

"Just with the people over there," Stephanie replied, pointing at the reception desk.

"Thanks, Stephanie."

Angela went over to the desk and briefly talked with the woman on duty.

"Are you two okay staying here?" she asked, when she came back to the seating area.

"We'll be fine," said Alex.

Angela smiled then made her way through the double doors into the interior of the hospital.

"So have you thought about what we're going to tell Marino?" asked Stephanie.

"Only that it needs to be the same as what we just told my dad," Alex replied.

"Can you remember all that?"

"Let's hope so," he said, with a wink.

They both saw Marino as she entered the reception area.

"How are you both?" she asked when she reached them. "How's your dad, Alex?"

"He's fine, they're looking after him, and my mom just went in to see him."

"Okay, I need to talk to him briefly too. I need to chat with you two as well, so don't go anywhere."

She went over to the reception desk then was directed through the double doors to where Andrew was being treated.

"Do we tell her about Henderson?" said Stephanie.

"We'll have to play it cool, see what she knows."

"Do you think we can trust her?"

"I hope so, but I can't be certain. Let's get a drink and snack from the vending machine."

BY THE TIME they sat back down, Marino emerged through the double doors. She walked over to where they were sitting.

"Well, your dad seems to be in good hands, Alex," she said. "I've asked for a private room where we can talk. Come this way."

She took Alex and Stephanie into a small room

adjacent to the reception area that appeared to be used as a coffee break room by the hospital staff members. There was a small kitchen area and the room had several chairs placed around a long table.

"I've asked that we aren't disturbed," said Marino as she sat down on one of the chairs.

She gestured for Alex and Stephanie to take a seat. They sat down on the chairs on the opposite side of the table.

"So," she began. "I guess it's time that you two told me what's been going on."

Alex and Stephanie managed to weave a convincing tale about how they'd rescued Andrew. Since they'd been linked to a suspected break-in at Castlewood Dynamics, they admitted to Marino that they'd been there. However, this was when they'd been attempting to collect Andrew's laptop on the day that Robert died. Marino mentioned that Sandy had confirmed their presence at the offices anyway. Alex and Stephanie convinced Marino that Veronica simply concocted the break-in story too since she knew that they were suspicious of her. Fortunately, Marino seemed to have no inkling that Alex and Stephanie might have been at the Castlewood mansion or at the lab in the basement of the headquarters.

"You should have thought about contacting me right away," said Marino.

"We did," Alex replied.

"You did?"

"I mean we did think about it but thought you'd be too busy."

"Then when we finally decided that we really needed your help," added Stephanie, "we couldn't

reach you on the phone so we went to your office.
That's when we met Officer Henderson."

"He was supposed to be taking us to see you," Alex
continued. "Then in the car we saw the real
destination was out in the woods. We had no idea
what it meant but took a chance that it was where my
dad was being held prisoner."

Marino nodded.

"We've been tracking business dealings and
trading on the stock market by someone with
connections to Castlewood Dynamics for quite a
while," she explained. "We've also been investigating
some of the companies that were associated with
Castlewood, mostly related to things that Veronica
was involved in. Robert Castlewood's death was also
viewed as suspicious."

Alex glanced over at Stephanie before he spoke
again.

"Veronica said that she had connections in the
police department. That some officers were delaying
the investigation into the car crash."

"A few things have emerged during the course of
our investigation, but I'm afraid I can't tell you
anything else."

"And Henderson?" asked Stephanie.

"I'm sorry," Marino replied. "I can't tell you any
more about that either. So what happened after you
saw the map showing where your dad might be being
held prisoner?"

Alex and Stephanie took turns explaining what
had happened on their journey through the woods
and when they'd reached the mine before escaping
with Andrew.

"And you say that the last time you saw Veronica

she was in the woods?" said Marino.

"Yes, she was unconscious when we left her there," Alex replied. "We knew those guys were coming to pick her up and they had guns too."

"Then we saw the van later racing away in the opposite direction on the highway," added Stephanie. "If they saw us in that guy's car they didn't care."

Marino shook her head.

"No, we think they went to a private airfield where Castlewood Dynamics have a number of different aircraft, planes as well as helicopters. We checked it out and one of the planes is missing."

"Where did she go?" asked Alex.

"We don't know yet. They didn't file a flight plan. She's probably over the border in Mexico but she won't stay there for long. She's more likely to go to a different country further from the U.S. She could be in hiding for a while."

"Will she come back?" said Stephanie.

"Probably not willingly. There's a lot of evidence regarding major crimes that she and her associates may be implicated in. It could take a long time to bring it all to trial and if she's in a country without an extradition treaty with the States she could well be gone for years."

"What about the Castlewood Dynamics?" Alex asked.

"It's been shut down for now and the employees are staying at home. However, as you know there are numerous branches overseas, partner companies in other countries, and others that Castlewood has shares in that many of us don't even know about."

"And she'll have the best lawyers too," Stephanie

pointed out.

"That's right," said Marino. "I don't think Veronica will be home any time soon but we'll do our best."

Alex's phone vibrated. He took it from his pocket but the message was just a promotional text from the phone company. Marino glanced at Alex's phone.

"Is that a new app, Alex?"

"What?"

"On your phone."

"Oh, yeah," Alex replied, trying to keep his cool. "It's just a game."

"I haven't seen that one before," said Marino. "But then again there are so many apps these days it's hard to keep up."

She stood up from her seat.

"Okay, I'd better go. I hope your dad's feeling better soon."

She walked over to the door and opened it for Alex and Stephanie before following them out into the reception area.

"I'll keep in touch but contact me if you remember anything else that you think might be helpful with the investigation."

"We will," said Stephanie.

"Bye," Alex added.

Marino smiled, then turned and walked toward the hospital's exit.

"That was a close one," said Stephanie, once Marino was well out of earshot. "Do you think she believed us?"

"About the app?"

"About everything."

"She seemed to," Alex replied. "After all, who'd

believe the truth anyway?"

They both laughed then went to check in with Andrew and Angela.

Chapter Twenty-One
Inventing The Future

TWO WEEKS LATER, Alex and Stephanie were watching TV at his house. The news was about to start, following some commercials. Alex's parents were visiting the hospital for Andrew's follow up treatment. Officer Marino had visited the house several times to check in on Andrew and to provide updates on the ongoing investigation. She'd explained how the police department, along with the FBI, was very busy both at the mine and in the facility in the depths of the Castlewood Dynamics headquarters. On her most recent visit Marino had revealed that Lewis and Palmer had been arrested, although Veronica's whereabouts were still unknown.

"So I guess Lewis and Palmer must have found Veronica near the dirt road, just after we left," said Stephanie.

"Yeah," Alex replied. "If they were heading to a

plane to get her out of the country, that would explain why they were driving so fast when we saw the van on the road in the woods. It sounds like she got away safely but they weren't so lucky."

"I wonder where she is now?"

"Who knows? Maybe there'll be something on the news."

"Hey," said Stephanie. "It's on."

"INVESTIGATIONS CONTINUE INTO Castlewood Dynamics, one of Silicon Valley's leading technology corporations," the news anchor began. "Operations by the police department and the FBI have focused on the company headquarters in San Jose as well as at a previously unknown research facility outside the city. Investigations by local law enforcement agencies are also taking place overseas at other Castlewood Dynamics offices and with several of Castlewood's subsidiaries and partner companies. Further arrests have been made although the company CEO Veronica Castlewood remains at large."

The news story primarily concerned the revelations about the company's business dealings. Much of the information was derived from evidence provided by the police department about the company's operations, corruption, and insider stock market trading. The police had learned much of this crucial information from the documents Stephanie had hurriedly emailed from the lab at the mine. Castlewood Dynamics remained temporarily closed down pending further investigation.

"Ms. Castlewood's lawyer spoke with reporters earlier today outside the company's headquarters," said the news anchor.

The image on the TV shifted to show Veronica's lawyer outside the Castlewood Dynamics offices. Reporters surrounded him, firing questions regarding recent developments, although the lawyer wasn't very forthcoming. Most of his answers were non-committal or simply sidestepped the reporters' questions.

"You can rest assured that we will be fighting these baseless allegations with the force of the law," he said as the press conference drew to a close. "Ms. Castlewood has done nothing wrong, but will remain outside the United States while the investigation continues."

"How long do you think she'll be out of the country?" said a reporter standing near the front.

"That will depend on the process of the investigation. I'm unable to speculate on that issue."

"And where is Ms. Castlewood currently located?" the same reporter asked.

"I'm afraid I can't comment on that," said the lawyer. "Thank you, ladies and gentlemen."

He abruptly brought the press conference to a close and pushed his way through the crowd to a waiting car as the reporters continued to ask him questions.

"Well, he didn't say too much, did he?" said Alex.

Before Stephanie could answer, the screen was suddenly filled with static. Alex and Stephanie were astonished as a familiar face appeared on the TV.

"Alexander!" Stephanie exclaimed.

"You're alive!" said Alex.

"Yes," said Alexander, smiling. "You could say that reports of my death have been greatly exaggerated."

"But the door breaking down," Alex said. "And those shots."

"And the blood," added Stephanie.

"I know," said Alexander, sighing. "Please accept my apologies. Like I told you, for me it had all happened before, when I was your age, Alex."

"We thought you were dead," said Alex.

"Yes, I'm sorry about that," said Alexander. "I had to do something dramatic to get your attention. I know how hard it was to stay on track and trust me, especially as things seemed to be happening differently to what I was telling you. You were definitely wavering by that point, wondering if you could change things or if it was all predetermined. My death seemed to be the only way to shake things up when I sent you the mine's coordinates."

"So was everything fake?" Stephanie asked. "Those images from the future?"

"The technology that you saw all exists," replied Alexander. "Fortunately, it's not all controlled by Castlewood Dynamics. I'm sorry I lied and only fed you limited information, but it was necessary. I was asking you to prevent a possible course of events. But I still had to make sure that you completed your mission so that Veronica's plans were defeated."

"So was the future ever really in danger?" asked Stephanie.

"Especially if you were deliberately misleading us all along," Alex added.

Alexander shook his head.

"Oh, it was in danger. If I hadn't sent the messages to get you to save Dad, Veronica would have won. Alex, you'd never have embarked on the mission, or even believed yourself capable of it, without my initial message from the future."

Alex thought for a moment.

"So is this knowledge of the future allowed? I mean, every book I've read or movie that I've seen says that's dangerous."

"Don't worry," said Alexander. "Now that you've defeated Veronica, the two of you will one day become partners and found a technology company together."

"Really?" asked Stephanie, excitedly.

"Yes, really," Alexander replied.

"What sort of things will we make?" said Alex.

Alexander smiled.

"You'll invent the technology that made this whole adventure possible in the first place. However, you shouldn't have any detailed knowledge of what's to come. That would be cheating."

He winked at them.

"The app on your phone will disappear soon, but it should still be on there for a few days. And now I have to say goodbye. Thank you for all your help."

Before Alex and Stephanie could ask any more questions, the image of Alexander vanished from the TV screen.

"So that's it?" said Stephanie. "He's gone for good?"

"Looks that way," Alex replied. "I don't think we'll hear from him again."

He looked down at the icon on his phone.

"You know, we should really study this app in more detail while we still can. We've been using it so much but we have no real idea how it works."

"Yeah," Stephanie agreed. "I'm curious about that

as well."

They stood up from the couch.

"I know this whole thing has been just insane," said Stephanie, as they walked toward the basement steps. "But don't you feel strange that we have to create the technology so that everything that happened could really happen?"

She shook her head.

"Even that sentence sounds crazy. You know what I mean though, right?"

"Yeah," Alex replied. "It is really weird, but then again, none of this ever made much sense, did it?"

They both laughed before heading down to the workshop in the basement. It would take some time, but they were about to begin work on the inventions that would in many ways shape their future.

About the Author

Simon was born in Derbyshire, England and has lived in Calgary since 1990.

He is the author of *The Alchemist's Portrait, The Sorcerer's Letterbox, The Clone Conspiracy, The Emerald Curse, The Heretic's Tomb, The Doomsday Mask, The Time Camera, The Sphere of Septimus,* and *Flashback.* Simon is also the author of *The Children's Writer's Guide*, a contributor to *The Complete Guide to Writing Science Fiction Volume One*, and has written many nonfiction books for younger readers.

Simon offers programs for schools, is an instructor with the University of Calgary and Mount Royal University and offers services for writers, including editing, writing workshops and coaching, plus copywriting for the business community.

Find Simon at http://simon-rose.com/

CPSIA information can be obtained at www.ICGtesting.com
Printed in the USA
LVOW11s0531130416

483327LV00001B/1/P